WHAT READERS are saying about Faith Wood's *Scent of Unfinished Business:*

"*Not sure how Wood does it, but she did it again with her new book! As always, I couldn't put it down!*"

—SANDY S.

"*A great cover is the first thing I look at when deciding on a new book, and I gasped when I saw Wood's. That made her book a 'must have. Didn't disappoint! Wonderful!*"

—MARSHA DILLARD

"*If you like great mystery writers, you're going to love Wood's books! Her newest book is no exception, and the Scent of Unfinished Business had me from the first page!*"

—LISA PAGE

"*I'll make this short and sweet. Read it. You won't be disappointed!*"

—ADAM HASSINGLER

"*I've read all of Wood's books, and couldn't wait to add the Scent of Unfinished Business to my collection. Fabulous!*"

—C. ARBOGHAST

SCENT

OF

UNFINISHED

BUSINESS

SCENT

OF

UNFINISHED

BUSINESS

FAITH WOOD

Inspiring Minds Media
British Columbia, Canada

DEDICATION

To all of my readers . . . I appreciate you!

Chapter I

There's a lot to be said for taking time. Time to think. Time to reassess. Time to figure out stuff long forgotten, but still taking its toll. The problem with that is there never seems to be answers to questions purposely buried as secret and inaccessible. Even so, when Colbie decided to take such time, she quickly figured out introspection wasn't all it was cracked up to be.

She supposed it shouldn't have bothered her when she stepped away from her investigation firm without fanfare. Of course, there was the possibility she set that scenario by always insisting on going it alone without recognition or favor from the men in her life. Still—there was a sting when she closed the door for the last time with no one to say goodbye.

Her life back then?

A rearview mirror thing.

It was strange, too—she never considered Ryan would hold her decision against her. When she first broached the subject with him while in Geneva after their last case, he seemed to be on board. Kevin, as well—especially since they decided to keep the business going during Colbie's absence. Was there a chance of changing her mind? Maybe.

But, she really didn't think so.

Returning to the States was a decision she didn't hesitate to make—after all, she missed the familiarity of family, old haunts, and friends who made her feel whole. But, as Colbie sat on the front steps of her Seattle bungalow watching a neighbor kid shank a soccer ball into his mom's flower bed, she couldn't disregard the newly surfacing tug of adventure.

It had been a long time.

Maybe I need a change of scenery, she thought as she watched the boy being hauled inside his house, Mom keeping a firm grasp on his arm.

Decision made.

CHAPTER 2

*T*bashi Abnal stared at the body, its skin cold, ashen, and stippled by ant bites, the face all but destroyed. It didn't take a genius to figure out it had been there awhile, especially since both eyes were nothing but empty sockets. "Did you notify the authorities?"

"Not yet—we just found it."

It was definitely a crippling situation no archaeological dig wanted—or, needed. The amount of down time and damage to reputation could be catastrophic, considering potential circumstances—but, if it turned out some poor sot took a wrong turn, the story would garner only a second or two on local news—maybe. If it turned out otherwise?

Something he couldn't risk by being negligent.

"Call the authorities," he ordered as he took a final look at the body.

"They'll want to speak with you . . ."

"I know. But, I have nothing to say to interest them . . ."

Two weeks passed since the neighbor kid was grounded for trashing his mom's flowers and, when choosing where to land, there was one thing of which Colbie was certain—no snow. Ice. Temps below sixty. As beautiful as Geneva and Seattle were, it was time to experience something completely different—a place where she could set course for the next years of her life without the frenetic life of the city.

So, when she found the perfect little rental close to the Calakmul Biosphere Reserve in Mexico, she couldn't resist. Little more than one room and somewhat primitive, she was pleased she had funds to rent something a bit more upscale— but, not by much.

Mosquito netting surrounded the bed, and there were amenities such as electricity and water, but that was about it. Still, to her, it was exactly what she needed—and, it wasn't far to the Biosphere Reserve. So? When the need for a restaurant hit?

Doable.

Besides, it was only for a month or two, and then it would be back to Seattle to figure out what she wanted to make of her life over the age of forty.

Weekly trips to the Calakmul Biosphere Reserve kept her in everything she needed, plus offering the opportunity to catch up on news and check her emails. Still, the Internet was spotty at best, and she didn't like the feeling of being out of touch—at least, not all the time. There was a part of her wanting to be in the know, and it was on her second trip to the reserve she learned of a body found at the archaeological dig near the Great Pyramid.

Turned out it wasn't some poor sot, after all.

She listened as a young reporter for a Mexico City television station recounted how and when the body was found with no supposition of what happened. Fortunately, she knew enough Spanish to get by and, so far, there was no language barrier. As she continued to listen, however, she realized she had much to learn.

"A well-known, United States archaeologist, Professor Richard Sanderson, was found dead at the Calakmul Great Pyramid. Supervising a nearby dig for several years, the professor was involved in directing several excavations within the ruins. Authorities are investigating."

That was it.

It would be foolish to think such a tidbit didn't pique Colbie's interest—it did. *I was planning to explore tomorrow,* she thought as she checked her cell for messages. *Maybe it's time I check out Calakmul . . .*

And, that was all it took.

She put aside what she knew was best—at least for a while—to chase a story that didn't concern her.

Although used to the damp of Seattle, it was nothing like the cloaking humidity of the Mexican jungle. Howler monkeys sounded off as Colbie ventured away from the main Mayan pyramid to a spot she could sit, relax, and people watch. Always one of her favorite pastimes, she enjoyed being inconspicuous as she noted body language of those walking by not noticing she was paying attention.

Water in hand, she chose a bench on the far, southwest side of the pyramid, cooling her face with it as she sat. A man—probably in his late thirties—stood, offering an obligatory hello before spotting something more interesting than she.

Watching, she noticed a slight limp in his left leg as he halted abruptly, a woman walking in front of him without a glance. *Perhaps he's on his own mission of self-discovery*, Colbie thought, curiously tracking his movements as he disappeared into the group of visitors.

Once out of sight, a weak, electrical twinge coursed through her—the familiar tingle of intuition. Closing her eyes, she tried to tune in, but there were too many people to be specific. She watched as her mind's eye ramped up a movie—one she was clearly meant to view—and, within moments, symbols began circling. A small statue. Blue paint. A pond.

Then, a whisper. "You stand at the platform of the Kingdom of the Snake . . ." Quietly, she waited, hoping for more.

Nothing.

Opening her eyes, she scanned the area to see if anyone were near—close enough for her to hear a whisper.

No one.

"Colbie? Colbie Colleen?"

She turned toward the voice, stunned anyone knew her name. "Damion?"

Suddenly, he pulled her up into a bear hug anyone would enjoy. "I can't believe it! What the hell are you doing here?" He held her at arm's length. "You look great!"

Although she was shocked to see the detective from Savannah, she had the presence of mind to ask about the whisper. "Did you say something to me before you called my name?"

"No. In fact, I nearly ran into the bench because I was looking the other direction . . ." He paused, still not believing she was in front of him. "So—what are you doing here?"

Colbie grinned, then sat again on the bench, patting the spot beside her. "You first . . ."

Damion matched her smile, then sat. "Well—there's not much to it, really. I've always wanted to see the Mayan ruins, and I had some vacation time coming. So, here I am!" He looked at her, his smile fading to something more serious. "What about you . . ."

So, for the next hour they chatted, each recounting time since they last saw each other a few years prior. It was then Colbie lost the love of her life and everything derailed, leaving her to pick up pieces of her shattered soul.

Finally, with a promise to meet for dinner the next evening at a small restaurant in the Reserve, they parted, each considering their coincidental meeting.

Each thinking it was just plain weird.

CHAPTER 3

As soft candlelight illuminated Colbie's face, Damion couldn't help admiring. Beauty aside, there was something about her he appreciated and, ever since they met in Savannah, he thought it would be nice to meet again.

Maybe spend a little time together.

"I have to admit—you were the last person I thought I'd run into!" He thanked the server as he placed two beers in front of them, waiting to continue conversation until they had a bit more privacy.

Colbie watched as he squeezed lime into his beer, then rub it on the rim of the frosted glass. "Honestly, I never gave a thought to meeting anyone I knew, let alone you!"

Damion raised his glass. "To serendipity . . ." He waited until Colbie took her first sip. "Tell me about Geneva . . ."

So, for the next two hours they chatted and, for the first time since Brian's passing, Colbie felt comfortable in her own skin. "After that, I realized it was time for me to move on . . ."

"I don't know—I have trouble believing you're giving up the investigation biz. Maybe you just need a break . . ."

Colbie nodded. "You might be right—I have to admit, when I heard they found a body close to the pyramid, the first thing I did was schedule a trip so I could check it out."

"See? I knew it!"

"Well—don't get too excited. I didn't find out anything— I wasn't even sure if I were in the right section of the grounds."

"Didn't they have it roped off?"

"Nope—no authority presence, whatsoever."

Damion was quiet for a minute, thinking. "That doesn't make sense. For a professor? I don't think so . . ."

"I thought the same thing—on the other hand, though, I don't know their customs. Maybe they give a professor of archaeology the same treatment as anyone else . . ."

"From the States? I doubt it—if there were foul play, you can bet someone will squawk about it."

"Maybe they have . . ." She too, was quiet, thinking about Professor Richard Sanderson. "It feels weird to be so close to an investigation without having my fingers in it . . ."

"I know." Damion took a sip of beer, then focused on the lovely woman across from him. "What do you see?"

"What do you mean?"

"Well, if I recall correctly, you have the gift . . ."

Colbie laughed as their server returned with homemade chips, and salsa. "The gift?"

"You know what I mean. Have you had any . . ."

"Visions?"

"Yes. I wasn't sure what to call them . . ."

"That's okay—sometimes, I'm not sure what to call them!" She paused. "But, the answer to your question is yes. When I was as Calakmul, I tried to tune in . . ."

"And?"

"It was interesting—nothing seemed to go together."

Damion was quiet for a moment as Colbie clearly recalled what she viewed in her intuitive mind. "What did you see," he finally asked.

"A statue, blue paint, and a pond . . ."

"You're right—I can see why you think they don't go together. But, they must—or, you wouldn't be seeing them. Is that how it works?"

Colbie smiled, enjoying his interest in her. "Yep—pretty much. Many times, I don't have any idea what they're about—especially when I'm at the beginning stages of an investigation."

"But, they're always a consideration, aren't they?"

She nodded. "Yes . . ."

Damion thought he noticed a tinge of regret in her voice. "Would you rather not have your abilities?"

Colbie sat forward in her chair, elbows on the table, chin resting on her clasped hands. "In all the years I've been working with my abilities, no one has ever asked me that question . . ."

"Well?"

"No—they're always a comfort. They have been since I was a kid . . ."

Damion would have liked to know more, but he didn't want to intrude on her privacy.

Change of topic.

"How long are you going to be here," he asked, catching the server's attention with a nod—moments later, he arrived with the check. Colbie eyed him, signaling she didn't expect him to pay for her meal—but, to no avail.

"Maybe another month—then, I'll head north."

"Back to Seattle?"

"Probably—I'm kind of leaving it to the last minute to decide."

"Then, that tells me you're standing at a crossroads . . ."

"Crossroads?"

"Yeah—what you're going through makes me wonder if you feel a part of you is missing, and you're trying to find it. If that's the case . . . is a month or two enough?"

Colbie cocked her head, not taking her eyes from him—his was a question she really didn't want to answer.

Instantly, Damion understood. "I'm sorry—that was too personal."

Colbie shook her head. "No—it wasn't. I just don't know the answer—maybe a month isn't enough. But, I guess I won't know until the time comes to make a finite decision."

"You'll do what's right for you," he agreed.

They fell into a comfortable silence, broken only by what Damion considered a great idea. "While you're here, why don't we do a little investigating into Professor Richard Sanders?"

"Seriously?"

"Why not?"

Colbie wasn't sure what to say—if she agreed, it might send a message she didn't want delivered. On the other hand—a little snooping and poking around couldn't hurt. "Well . . ."

"Oh, c'mon—it'll be fun!"

"Don't you have to get back to work?"

Damion shook his head. "Nope—I'm actually on a sabbatical, of sorts."

"Of sorts?"

"Yep . . ."

It was clear he didn't want to elaborate, and Colbie didn't want to ask. "Okay . . ."

"So—what do you say? We do our own investigation?"

As Colbie started to answer, she couldn't believe what was about to come out of her mouth. "I'm in . . ."

"Do you have it?"

"No . . ." It was the answer he knew would get him in hot water. But, to lie?

More than trouble.

David Ramskill focused on the man, disgust settling in his eyes. "No?" He waited a moment in case he changed his answer.

"No—it wasn't there."

"Bullshit! It has to be! I know for a fact he kept it in the safe . . ."

"The safe wasn't there, either . . ."

"What?"

The younger man didn't say anything, waiting for the onslaught of curse words to cease. When Ramskill hired him, he had no idea what he was getting into and, right then, he had no idea of how to get out. "I don't know—all I know is I went through every inch of his place, and the damned thing isn't there."

The two men sat, each weighing ramifications of their first failure. "Then," Ramskill finally commented, "that means there's another player . . ."

Dismissing the young man who failed his mission, he privately vowed to hire someone who may be better suited to the job—although, finding one he could trust would be tough. Those within the archaeological community regarded Professor Richard Sanderson the godfather of digs and research, placing Ramskill in a position of alienating colleagues if anyone learned of his duplicity.

First meeting in grad school, Sanderson and Ramskill transformed the archaeology department of their university after both received doctorates, choosing to remain at their alma mater for the initial years of their professional lives. A few years turned into ten and, after the first decade, they parted ways, Sanderson opting to live a life of adventure. "It's what I've always wanted to do," he confided to Ramskill prior to announcing his departure.

"Then, you should do it, my friend . . ."

"I have ideas no one's considered and, if I stay, my freedom to discover will be lost . . ."

And, that was it. For Professor Richard Sanderson? New adventures. New discoveries.

A new life.

"Okay—where do you want to start?" Damion pushed his iced tea to the middle of the table as he opened a white, unlined tablet.

"Well—I think the first thing we need to get a grip on is Richard Sanderson. All we know is he was a professor of archaeology, but we really don't have any idea of why he was in Calakmuh . . ."

Damion nodded. "Obviously, some sort of research— when I Googled him last night, his name was everywhere when it came to ancient ruin sites . . ."

"Then you had better luck than I," Colbie laughed. "I tried for a few hours to get a good connection . . ." She paused. "So, what about him? Age?"

"On the downhill slide to forty—and, he was a well-known and respected researcher. His work is admired in archeology and anthropology circles . . ."

"What did he study?"

"Interesting stuff—ancient cultures and societies. And, apparently, he commissioned to work with researchers here."

"At the pyramid?"

"Yes—I found a few articles about his finding a small statue years ago, but nothing else."

Instantly, Colbie recalled what she saw while sitting on the Mayan pyramid granite bench. "Remember my vision at the site?"

Damion thought for a moment until the light went on. "That's right! A statue . . ."

Colbie nodded. "Maybe it has something to do with the murder . . ."

"Murder? Possibly—but, for now and since we have nothing to go on, let's file that thought away until evidence leads us to it."

Colbie grinned, thinking how different his approach was from hers. *If Brian heard you say that*, she thought, *he'd laugh his ass off!*

Damion caught her grin. "What's so amusing?"

"Well, it's clear you and I do things differently—I was just thinking Brian would chuckle at your 'cop' approach."

"I take it my approach isn't how you go about it . . ."

"Well, in many ways, it is. But, I always give credence to my intuitive abilities and, since I had a vision of a small statue, perhaps we should explore that lead first . . ."

Damion hesitated, knowing the way he tackled a case worked well—he also knew Colbie's take on it would be valuable. "Okay—I'm game. Where do you want to start?"

"The statue—did you happen to find out where he found it?"

"Yep—a ruin site in Georgia."

"Georgia? You're from there—had you heard of it?"

"No—and, it wasn't exactly what I was expecting."

"Did the article mention if the statue had anything to do with his current research?"

"Nope . . ." Damion paused, getting a good look at the way Colbie worked through a case. "I have the link . . ." Seconds later, it arrived on her cell.

"Thanks—I'll read it later. For now, though, I think we need to find out exactly who Richard Sanderson was—married?

"No—and, no kids."

"That doesn't surprise me—I imagine being gone on a dig would make it tough for a marriage to survive."

Damion laughed, then reached for his tea. "Or, maybe it's the other way around!"

"Either way, we need to find out what people close to him knew about his research . . ."

"Check. Divvy up the duties?"

"Yep . . ."

For the next hour, each laid out a plan to obtain additional information about the archaeologist, as well as explore current and past colleagues. Agreeing to meet in a few days, they parted, both privately wondering if they made the right decision to investigate on the Q.T.

We'll know soon enough, she thought as she stepped into her cottage late that evening, thinking about what she needed to accomplish. First on her list?

The Georgia connection.

CHAPTER 4

*A*s memorial services go, Richard Sanderson's was somewhat uneventful. Only a handful of mourners graced the pews and, an hour after it began, they filed from the church hoping not to appear as if they had things to do.

"I can't believe this happened . . ." Peyton Maxwell's tears spilled, the thought of not seeing Sanderson more than she could bear. "I met him while I was a grad student, and we just kind of . . ."

"Hit it off?"

"Well, yes . . ."

"Well, I'm certain my brother felt the same way about you . . ." Emma Sanderson's voice was tender and gentle like a grandma speaking to her favorite granddaughter.

"Does anyone know what happened?"

Emma shook her head, recalling the difficulty trying to get information from the Mexican government. "As far as I know, they don't know anything . . ."

Peyton swiped at her tears, attempting to pull herself together. "But, that doesn't make any sense—he didn't have a heart condition, or any other illness."

"You're right about that—Richard was as healthy as they come. In fact, he insisted on it . . ."

"Then what . . ." Peyton's voice caught as a new well of tears filled.

As much as Emma hated to admit it, there was a strong possibility they'd never know the truth—but, imparting such information to a young woman who was obviously enamored with her brother?

Probably not smart.

Moments later, tissues in hand, each went her own way, thinking thoughts both preferred to keep to themselves. Emma promised to keep Peyton apprised about any changes in the situation, knowing full well she wouldn't be talking to her any time soon.

If, at all.

Within the first three days of working her unofficial investigation, Colbie knew one thing—to investigate the Georgia connection properly, she had to go there. To do a thorough investigation, she couldn't begin while sitting on the tiny porch of her south-of-the-border cottage with no Internet.

"What do you think about heading back to your home state?"

"Are you kidding?" Damion switched his cell to the other ear. "This is a bad connection—I can barely hear you. Did you say you want to head to Georgia?"

Colbie laughed, anticipating his response. "Yep! You heard me! We can't do a proper investigation here—you know that."

"Well . . ."

"So, if you don't want to leave yet, I'll go. I think we need to track the statue—you know, when he acquired it, where, and all of that . . ."

Clearly, she was right, but Damion wasn't quite so quick to change his plans for something of which he knew little. After all, they weren't officially on the investigation—still, since he was the one suggesting it in the first place, he'd look like an idiot if he declined. "I'm in . . . do you want me to make reservations since I have a better Internet connection?"

"Perfect—I don't have much with me, so I can pick up and go . . ."

With a promise to ring her back within the hour, Damion clicked off with more than a thought or two about what just happened. The whole point of his visiting Calakmuh was for a little relaxation—what he didn't tell Colbie?

It wasn't his idea.

You see, it was nearly a year prior when Detective Damion Dellinger snapped. While understandable, it didn't set well with the higher ups and, after his second episode of unstable behavior, the suggestion came down from on high. "You need to take a little time off . . ."

That was it.

He chose not to make a big deal of it, leaving with the option of returning, but only upon proof of mental stability. Right then, he wasn't so sure he wanted to get into it again and, when he mentioned it to Colbie, he didn't really think she'd take the ball, and run.

I should have known . . .

Blairsville, Georgia was a sleepy little town and, within the week, Colbie rented a room from a lovely elderly couple while Damion returned home to Savannah, nearly six hours away. Both agreed it wasn't necessary for them to be within close proximity and, with a strong Internet, they could communicate easily.

"The first place I want to go is Brasstown Bald," she told him the evening she got settled.

"I've heard of that place, but I've never been there—now, I have a reason to go!" He didn't think about how his comment sounded until it came out of his mouth.

"Really?" Instantly, she regretted the playful banter.

"You know what I mean!"

"I do—I'm just giving you a hard time." A pause. "So—back to business. It seems there's quite a rivalry between the scholarly types and free thinkers . . ."

"Explain . . ."

"Well—there's a strong contingent on the side of possibility the Maya emigrated to Georgia."

"Not the other way around?"

"Do you mean they possibly could have emigrated from Georgia to the Yucatan?"

"Exactly! Whose to say they weren't here first?"

Colbie was quiet, thinking about his question. "I don't suppose there's any way to really know . . ."

"Why do they think they were here?"

"Because of the terraced mountain formations, and one guy wrote about the possibility of the site's being the fabled city of Yupaha . . . which, as I understand it, de Soto failed to find in 1540."

"Never heard of it . . ."

"Neither had I—but, I suppose if you lived in these parts for a long time, it's stuff of legend."

"Okay—I'll take your word for it. What's next?"

Colbie scribbled a note to herself. "Like I said, I'll head to Brasstown Bald to see the terraced formation for myself. Who knows? Maybe I'll tune in to something . . ."

"Check—I'll start researching Richard Sanderson from the time he was in college to now."

"What about family members?"

"A few that I could find, but, only Emma Sanderson—a sister five years older than Sanderson—lives close."

"Does she live in Georgia?"

"Yep—actually, only a few hours from you."

"Perfect! Do you have a contact number?"

Within seconds, a text notification of Emma Sanderson's address and home phone number sounded on her cell. "Got it—thanks!"

With that, they rang off, each agreeing to get in touch within a couple of days. In the meantime, Colbie was to contact Emma for a face-to-face while Damion learned as much as he could about Sanderson. Between the two of them?

We ought to come up with something . . .

"It won't be long until they come looking . . ." The well-dressed, stately man turned from gazing out the window. Acquiring the statue would be quite a coup—one which he planned to carry out ever since Sanderson made the archaeological find of the past fifty years. With the naked eye, it resembled nothing more than a small, granite statue, possibly of local, ancestral decent. To him?

The gateway to riches.

"You know Ramskill will search for it . . ." The young man with a wiry build and sandy hair watched him carefully, assessing everything.

"Yes—and, any pathetic attempt he makes will, undoubtedly, be thwarted. However, he will fail as he does with most things in life . . ." He turned his attention once again to something outside the window. "But, should they get too close . . ."

Neither said a word, his implication clear.

Moments of such clarity often places one in a harsh, unyielding light—one laying bare personal secrets as well as misguided ambition. Some recognize it. Some don't. But, to anyone who chose to look?

The sharp-dressed man wasn't the man he seemed.

Not even close.

Colbie pulled into a long lane, then parked in front of an unassuming, quaint farmhouse. Closing her eyes, she sat for a moment, trying to tune in on the person she was going to meet. *Short. Dark hair. A mole on her left cheek . . .*

Moments later, she stood on the front porch waiting for Emma Sanderson to answer her knock. With barely time to scan the area, the door opened with a comforting creak. "Colbie?"

"Yes! And, you must be Emma . . ."

Introductions out of the way, Richard Sanderson's sister led her to a small parlor, complete with lace curtains. "This reminds me of my grandmother's place," Colbie commented, accepting a glass of lemonade.

"Well, then, you must be a country girl—this property belonged to my great-grandmother!" Smiling, she made herself comfortable. "And, it's said I look just like her . . ." She pointed to the mole on her cheek. "I got this from her!"

"Genetics are an incredible thing, that's for sure!" Colbie eyed family pictures on the fireplace mantel. "Is that Richard?"

"Oh, yes—that was taken several years ago. Before he went to the Yucatan . . ."

"I know he was highly regarded within the academic community . . ."

"Well—he achieved a lot. It's hard to believe he won't have his entire life to satisfy his dream . . ."

"How old was he?" Of course, Colbie knew, but rehashing familiar information was perfect validation.

"Thirty-nine—he had his doctorate in archaeology and anthropology by the time he was twenty-six, and he spent a little over ten years teaching at the university level . . ."

"I remember reading about that . . ."

"Then, he needed to explore. You know, do things he wanted to do within the field . . ."

Colbie nodded. "I know exactly what you mean—I, too, sometimes feel drawn to pursue other things."

Emma leveled an inquiring and challenging look. "Then, why don't you?"

"Who knows? I still might!" Colbie grinned, then took a sip of her lemonade. "This is really good! Homemade?"

"You really are a country girl! I made it this morning . . ."

Colbie was quiet for a moment, gathering her thoughts. "So, you know why I'm here . . ."

Emma nodded. "You want to know about the statue . . ."

"Yes—from what I read, it was a quite the find."

"It was—Richard had offers from collectors, but he chose to turn them down. He said it wasn't about the money—and, I think he would have preferred it go to a museum." She paused. "But, that's obviously not going to happen . . ."

"What do you mean?"

Emma focused on Colbie with a contemptuous look. "It was stolen . . ."

"What?"

"They don't know exactly when, but it was soon after they found him at the site. He always kept it in a safe where he lived . . ."

"Where was that," Colbie interrupted.

"Compeche—he lived there for the last few years."

"How do you know it's gone? Maybe he changed the location to keep it safe . . ."

"Perhaps, but I doubt it. My brother was a creature of habit, and I know for a fact he bought a safe when he got down there."

"I'm afraid I still don't understand—how do you know the statue was stolen?"

Emma hesitated for a second, recalling the conversation she had with authorities. "They didn't find the safe . . ."

"You mean the whole thing was gone?"

"Yes—no sign of it." Again, she paused. "And, from what Richard told me, it wasn't tiny. It had to be fairly heavy . . ."

"So, the question becomes who had the means to walk out of your brother's place with a heavy safe, and not be detected . . ."

"Well, we don't know if he were detected, or not. The authorities don't seem too interested—in fact, they couldn't wait to get my brother's body out of their hair."

"And, out of their jurisdiction . . ."

"Exactly . . ."

So, before she realized it, Colbie was back in investigation mode, completely immersed in the death of Professor Richard

Sanderson. After spending another couple of hours with his sister, she left with the thought no one really had any idea of what was going on. *There isn't an investigation brewing in the States*, she thought as she climbed into her rental.

By the time she left Emma, there was little doubt Richard Sanderson's untimely passing came to a close for most concerned.

Except Colbie.

CHAPTER 5

By the time she returned home, exhaustion met her at the door and, within minutes of her arrival, Colbie curled up in the antique chair by the window in her bedroom. It was a comfort reverting her to childhood—her grandmother's house in the northwest—a place of solitude when a cozy rain made her feel secure. Safe.

Accepted.

It was there—in that chair—she drifted into her shadow world, feeling its familiar comfort as she contemplated things about life most people don't want to entertain. In her personal shadow, things normally filled with grace and importance trended to the darker side when trying to figure out who she was, and where she was going—questions always causing her to misstep.

Some may call crossing the threshold into the shadow self an act of meeting one's demons—you know, wrestling with the devil, or experiencing a dark night of the soul.

Mid-life crisis.

For Colbie, it was a place she knew existed—yet, at times, it was something to which she remained willfully blind, refusing to accept the side of herself where she hoped pain, disappointment, and emotions wouldn't take advantage.

But, they did.

As she tried to regain life after Brian by wrapping her grief into a tidy, little package to be placed in the farthest recesses of her mind, her shadow self prompted thoughts of how she could have done more in their relationship. How she could have been kinder.

How she could have done a lot of things.

Closing her eyes, self-doubt inched into her soul as she began to question everything—the investigation. Damion.

Herself.

So, legs tucked beneath her in a chair rich with life, Colbie entertained thoughts of who she wanted to be. How she wanted to be. How she wanted to get there. As she learned in college psychology, man is less than he imagines himself—or, wants to be. Everyone, including her, carries a shadow closely held, forming something on which to falter, intended to barricade the most well-meant intentions.

Still, she thought as she sat in fading summer light, *no matter how well we understand, we hide our negative qualities. Not only from others . . .*

But, ourselves . . .

The following day, Brasstown Bald was nothing like Colbie expected—but, to be honest, she had no idea of what she wanted to find. Yes, she knew of the terraced mountains, but other than that? She wasn't sure if answers to her questions were right in front of her, or buried deeply in legend and wishful thinking. In any event, the trip she thought might be elucidating, yielded nothing as far as truth.

"Honestly—it was kind of a waste of time, and I could have sat on the porch with my laptop to find out the same thing."

"Was it cool?" Colbie's lack of enthusiasm when it came to the legend of the Maya being in Georgia was a surprise. *But,* Damion figured, *without having many people to talk to about it . . .*

"It was—but, I can't help thinking it really doesn't have anything to do with our investigation. It's simply an information source . . ." She paused, thinking of how to proceed. "What about you? Did you find anything out about any of Sanderson's colleagues?"

"If you mean did I dig up any dirt on them, the answer is no. But, if you mean did I find anyone warranting my attention? The answer is yes . . ."

"Really? Who?"

Damion paused as he flipped through his notes. "The main one is David Ramskill—there seems to be a train of thought he was jealous of Sanderson. But, as of now, it's nothing, but talk . . ."

"Maybe so—but, it's still worth checking out."

"Agreed—tomorrow I'll focus on Ramskill. He works at his alma mater university, so he should be fairly easy to track down . . ."

"Except that it's summer . . ."

Damion chuckled. "You're right—if I can't find him at the university, I'll try his home.'"

As Colbie listened to his matter-of-fact approach to their investigation, she couldn't help feeling sorry for him, wondering if he ever followed his gut. Although she couldn't see him, she was certain his notes were in order—probably by date, and time—as he followed their self-imposed trail. Even so, how he structured his life was none of her business, cueing her to think briefly about her own way of doing things. Although she recognized such organization is a good thing, she never could get on board no matter how hard she tried—that one time.

"Colbie?"

"I'm sorry—my mind wandered for a minute."

"I know the feeling—we were talking about David Ramskill . . ."

"Oh, yes—my gut tells me he's a player in all of this, so it's important we find him." Colbie paused. "Do you want to interview him, or shall I?"

"I'll take care of it, and send you my notes as soon as I have them in order . . ."

Colbie smiled, knowing her intuition about her quasi-partner was on target. "Perfect! In the meantime, I'm going to spend a little time getting in touch with a few of Sanderson's former students . . ."

"Good idea . . ."

"It's a crapshoot, but someone may have more than anecdotal or insignificant information. If that's the case, I want to hear everything . . .

It's a certain kind of person who can sit in front of a computer screen all day—and, Colbie Colleen wasn't one of them. After a morning of scouring the Internet, she had little to show for her efforts and, although she knew it wasn't, it felt like wasted time. Of course, there were myriad photos of university students, but unless she knew who she was trying to find?

Impossible.

It wasn't until she was ready to throw in the towel, did she think of Emma. *There had to be students at Sanderson's funeral*, she thought as she tapped her cell screen to life—within seconds, a connection.

Explaining the reason for her call, it didn't take Emma long to recall a young lady with long, blonde, curly hair. "There really weren't many people at the service—but, I do remember talking to a former student."

"Do you know her name?"

Emma hesitated. "Peyton—but, I don't know her last name . . ."

After another ten minutes, Colbie rang off, promising to keep in touch even though she knew anything she learned would go through a process—and, it didn't include family of victims. As much as she wanted to keep them in the loop, there was obvious, considerable risk in doing so—especially if preliminary information turned out to be inaccurate.

An hour into her renewed search? Pay dirt. "Peyton Maxwell," she murmured, though there was no one listening. "This has to be her . . ."

Firing off a quick text to Damion, it was only thirty minutes before she had the student's contact information. Twenty-four hours later?

A meeting with Peyton Maxwell.

Colbie extended her hand, offering a warm smile. "Thank you for meeting with me! I couldn't believe my luck when you said you were available today . . ."

The early-thirties archaeologist grinned. "I'm beginning to learn timing really is everything!"

Official introductions behind them, they sat on a park bench Colbie assumed was close to the young woman's home. "It's beautiful here," she commented. "I've been staying in Blairsville, but I'm thinking of moving a little closer to the city."

"Atlanta?"

Colbie laughed. "I have no idea—I haven't gotten that far yet! Wherever it is, though, it will be temporary. I'm only in Georgia for a short time . . ." She paused, her voice lowering, and serious. "So—I'm sure you're wondering why I asked to meet . . ."

"Well . . . yes."

"I'm sorry I didn't tell you more, but, as with all of my investigations, I don't like providing too much information before meeting . . ."

Peyton cocked her head, eyeing Colbie. "Investigations?"

"Yes—I'm investigating Professor Richard Sanderson's death and, when I talked to his sister, she indicated she spoke with you at his funeral service."

"What makes you think I know anything about him?"

In that moment, Colbie realized the beautiful Peyton Maxwell wasn't going to cough up information without a damned good reason. "Honestly, Peyton, I don't—I'm just getting started, and I'm trying to get a handle on what happened."

Again, Peyton eyed her, doubt creeping into her eyes. "Why me?"

"Like I said, Emma said she talked to you at the funeral— and, to me, you seem like a good place to start." Colbie paused, not waiting for her to answer. "If I recall correctly, Emma said you were one of his students . . ."

"Is this off the record?"

What an odd question, Colbie thought as she clicked her pen, ready to take notes. "Everything you tell me will be confidential . . ."

Peyton hesitated, still uncertain. "I don't know—I don't feel right about it. Emma said no one knows what happened to him, so I don't know what I can add. It was well over a year since I last saw him . . ."

As Peyton spoke, Colbie decided against taking notes, leaving everything the young woman said to memory. "I know he traveled extensively and was working on a dig in the Yucatan . . ."

"He worked that dig for several years—in fact, he rarely came home. When he did, we made it a point to connect . . ."

"I can only imagine the stories he had to tell—was he working with anyone else you knew on the dig?"

"Not really—I heard a couple of years ago Professor Ramskill was going to join him, but I don't know if that happened."

Colbie smiled, casually sitting back on the bench. "What's he like?"

"Richard, or Professor Ramskill?"

Colbie nodded. "Professor Ramskill—from what I read about Professor Sanderson's colleagues, Ramskill is a highly regarded archaeologist."

"Yes, and no—but, Professor Ramskill isn't as nice as Richard." Peyton blushed, realizing she telegraphed her relationship with the professor was on a first-name basis.

Colbie chose to ignore it. "What do you mean?"

"Only that his personality was the exact opposite . . ."

"Interesting—you mean the opposite of Sanderson's?" Purposely, she used the professor's first name, knowing it promoted a certain familiarity.

"Yes—Richard was kind, and genuinely interested in his students."

"What about Professor Ramskill?"

Peyton hesitated, thinking about the man who sent shivers up her spine. "I didn't know him too well—I had a few classes with him, and that was about it. And, it was several years ago . . ." She paused. "But, there's something about him that gave me the creeps—then, and now."

"Did Richard ever say anything about him?"

"No—not really. The only thing I remember was about a year ago . . ." Another pause. "Actually, now that I think about it, that was the last time I saw Richard . . ."

So, as Peyton Maxwell became more at ease while chatting, there was little doubt her relationship with Sanderson was more than friendship—something about which Colbie wanted to know more, yet she didn't want to put the skids on their conversation. "What do you remember," Colbie prompted.

"He said he didn't trust him—and, neither do I, although I don't know why. There's just something about him . . ."

"I know what you mean—kind of like a feeling you get when you know you need to stay away from someone."

"Or, something . . ."

"True—but, if Richard didn't trust him, and neither do you, I'll bet there are others who think the same thing." Colbie paused. "Can you think of anyone?"

Peyton thought for a moment, then shook her head. "No—the only person I remember seeing with Professor Ramskill was Nathan Moss."

"Who's he?"

"He was in grad school when I was undergrad—if Ramskill were around, it was a good bet Nathan would be standing in his shadow."

"I think I know what you mean—like a puppy who wants attention."

"That's right! Honestly, there was something pathetic about him—but, like I said, I don't know him, and I don't want to . . ."

"Did he give you a . . . creepy feeling?"

"Oh, yes—and, I wasn't the only one who didn't want to be around him. My friends felt the same way . . ."

And, there they sat—chatting as if they were old friends. By the end of their time together, going their separate ways, Colbie felt as if she had something to go on—finally. There was one thing about which she was quite certain when it came to the lovely Peyton Maxwell . . .

Nothing she said resembled the truth.

"I can't imagine why you requested a meeting—I'm sure we have little to discuss." Clifford Rasmussen didn't take his eyes from the man who stood in his office, refusing the courtesy of accepting an offered seat.

"Surely you heard . . ."

"Heard what?"

David Ramskill said nothing for a moment, wondering if he made an egregious error. If so, however, there was no turning back.

"The statue . . "

"What about it?"

"It's missing . . ."

"Oh, come now—how could it be missing? Richard didn't let it out of his sight!" Then, a thought. "And, David, if it truly is the case, how do you know?"

The first clue that Ramskill's being there was, indeed, a mistake.

"Well," he replied, backpedaling, "I don't, really. But, there hasn't been any mention of it since Sanderson cro . . ." He caught himself. "Died . . ."

"Did you honestly believe there would be? That statue is worth a fortune—I hardly think it's fallen into the hands of a nefarious soul."

Ramskill was quiet for a moment, disgusted by his colleague's arrogance. "If I recall, Clifford, you had an interest in that statue from the moment Sanderson discovered it . . ."

"Only from an archaeological perspective . . ." Although he didn't elaborate, Clifford Rasmussen found Ramskill's implication distasteful. Offensive. "What are you saying, David? Do you think I had something to do with its disappearance if, in fact, it is missing?"

"Of course not—but, if it's truly missing? It would have to be taken by someone knowing its worth—someone within our own field."

"Perhaps—unfortunately, we'll never know." He focused on Ramskill as if daring him to say more. "Is there anything else, David? I have a meeting in ten minutes . . ."

An intentional dismissal.

CHAPTER 6

Nathan Moss was an unassuming kind of guy—you know, the type who doesn't say much at parties, much preferring to stay on the periphery. By the end of his senior year in college, it was a given if he attended any event, within an hour of his arrival, he was out the door. "Too many people," he confided to his roommate. "Besides, I have nothing in common with any of them . . ."

Over-inflated self-importance? Perhaps. Even so, as an out-of-the-nest adult?

Life dealt more than one unforeseen blow.

Some say it was his intellect getting him into trouble, a sentiment often up for debate. For Nathan Moss, holding a job was iffy and, if asked, he'd tell anyone who'd listen everything was the other guy's fault. Never one to accept responsibility, it was a way of life employers—especially those in the academia arena—didn't handle particularly well. Still, not understanding such arrogance, they made allowances for him, many believing in his innate ability to do great things.

Especially David Ramskill.

As a student, Moss bordered on genius. Yet, there were family and friends wondering why he chose a double major of anthropology and archaeology—it certainly seemed he was capable of much more. But, those who knew him well were keenly aware of his darker, more introspective side. They commented it was the part of his personality enjoying delving into ancient, ritualistic cultures—the Mayans, in particular.

Such understanding, however, they kept to themselves.

Unfortunately, post-university years weren't particularly kind to the fledgling, on-the-fringe archaeologist. A few research positions worked out fairly well—until colleagues and supervisors caught unapologetic glimpses of the young man's dichotomous demeanor. In fact, a good friend suggested counseling to rid himself of personal demons—and, it was probably a good idea.

Except, according to Moss, he didn't have any.

It wasn't until his early thirties did he decide to join forces with someone—anyone—who would allow him to be himself. After a decade plus in the work force, it was painfully clear he wasn't cut out for playing well with others—so, when David Ramskill came knocking?

Things couldn't have been more perfect.

Although she didn't realize it at the time, Peyton Maxwell's conversation with Colbie Colleen opened what she thought were long-healed wounds. The truth was—although she didn't mention it at the time—she only showed up to Richard Sanderson's memorial service because she felt she should pay her respects. An obligation thing. Those few in Sanderson's inner circle would have found not doing so a slight against their relationship—even if it were long since disintegrated.

It began innocently enough, as do most budding relationships. After dipping her toes in the history major pool, Peyton didn't decide until her junior year she wanted to change to archaeology—for some reason, she was drawn to ancient cultures and the psychology of their rituals. But, it wasn't until she sat in on a lecture by Professor Richard Sanderson did she definitively decide to dump her major, doing a complete one-eighty into the realm of ruins.

Well, one thing led to another and, several years after Peyton graduated, her relationship with the professor ramped up—with the caveat, of course, they were to keep it on the Q.T. As a couple, they could've counted friends on one hand— something on which Sanderson insisted—and, it was an understanding that worked well.

Until there were fractures.

Was it the life Peyton wanted for herself?

Not really.

It was a realization creating contentious feelings between them and, when Sanderson left on a long-term archaeology project years earlier only to return periodically, dousing the torch was her first option. She was ready to do it, too . . .

If Sanderson hadn't gotten to it first.

In a brief, scrawling letter a year-and-a-half prior to his passing, he suggested she find someone who would be better suited to the life she wanted to live. At least, that was the gist—she stopped reading after the first couple of lines. For Peyton, it was a slap in the face with little regard for her feelings. Still, on the one occasion when he returned to the States, a year or so previous, they got together with the understanding it was purely professional. The long and short for Peyton Maxwell?

Being jilted wasn't an option.

By the end of the week, Colbie relocated to a short-term rental on the outskirts of Savannah—far enough away for a less-stressed life, yet still in close proximity to amenities, should she need them. Besides, she was familiar with the city, and there was a welcoming familiarity when she spent her first night there in two years.

After a quick bite to eat, she spread her notes on the kitchen table, reminding her of the neophyte stages of her career. *It's nice to know some things never change*, she thought as she opened her notebook. But, it wasn't until she flipped to the conversation with Peyton Maxwell did she entertain serious thoughts about the former student's relationship with Richard Sanderson. *There definitely was one*, she thought as she closed her eyes, ready to receive images. Slowing her breathing, she entered the world of her intuitive mind, once again relying on it to provide information she desperately needed.

It was when Colbie Colleen was young—thirteen, or so—she accepted she was different. However, that wasn't when she knew she had intuitive abilities—that happened at age six when she spouted off at the dinner table her uncle John was going to die the next day. It was, undoubtedly, a pronouncement causing great concern, one ultimately sending Colbie to her room to think about what she said.

Even so, she stuck to her premonition, refusing to admit she had what her parents termed 'an overactive imagination.' So, the following day when John Colleen dropped dead of a heart attack as he was climbing a ladder to clean the gutters, it came as a shock to the entire family.

Except Colbie.

From that time forward, premonitions became a way of life—and it was, unfortunately, a life filled with criticism, sarcasm, and bullying. Classmates couldn't quite grasp what she was talking about, and would-be friends decided to jump ship before getting started. For Colbie?

A lonely life.

It was then—sometime around eighth grade—she decided to immerse herself in her psychic abilities and, by the time she graduated high school, speaking to those who passed over was a breeze. She asked questions. They answered. It wasn't until years later, however, she toyed with the notion of using her abilities for the basis of her investigations business.

An idea that worked, the technique she devised to reach those on the other side was the same as the day she discovered it shortly after turning into her teens—she asked for a name, location, and a description of the killer, unsure of which she would get. It was like a formula—one never failing to provide what she needed.

Sinking deeper into meditation, she asked for Richard Sanderson to join her, inviting him to give her valid information regarding his untimely passing. A few moments later, she felt the energy next to her change, prompting her to ask the first question. Thanking him for joining her, she then got down to business. *Are you Richard?*

She waited, uncertain of how answers would come— sometimes, they were audible as if the person were right next to her. Other times, visions appeared and vanished in her mind's eye, and it was up to her to interpret, then verify. That evening?

It was like watching T.V.

Her eyelids fluttered as she viewed a path into what looked like a jungle. Then, suddenly, as if she were the subject of her vision, she was running, looking back over her left shoulder, eyes wide with terror and certain realization. Moments later?

Gone.

Experience advised her to wait for more images and, sometimes, it was worth it. That time?

Nothing.

Although slightly disappointed she didn't receive more, at least she had a starting point. One thing was becoming clear . . .

Richard Sanderson was murdered.

CHAPTER 7

"Thank you for meeting me, Professor Ramskill . . ." Damion smiled as they shook hands. "I'm surprised you're not off enjoying your summer vacation!"

"I should be," David laughed, "but, I'm teaching a new course beginning in August, and I need to be prepared. It'll be here sooner than I think . . ."

Damion scanned the professor's office, eyeing artifacts dating back to a world he couldn't imagine. "This . . . is incredible!" Slowly, he toured the room, careful not to touch. "Are all of these from the same place?"

"Most of them—I specialize in Mayan culture. A few, however, are from digs I was on in Egypt much earlier in my career . . ." He pointed to three shelves to Damion's right.

"It's amazing to look at something close up, and realize how old it is. I can't help but think of what life was like . . ."

The professor grinned. "Exactly why I decided to go into anthropology and archaeology—it's a story with no ending." He focused his attention on the detective. "Now . . . is it Detective Dellinger?"

Damion nodded. "Yep—but, I'm officially on sabbatical for the summer. I happened to be visiting the Yucatan when I heard about Professor Sanderson . . ." He paused. "Naturally, it piqued my interest . . ."

"Ah, yes—Richard. It's a shame . . ." He hesitated without looking at his visitor. "Do they have any idea of what happened?"

"As far as I know, there isn't much to go on . . ."

"That's what I heard, as well . . ."

"Oh? Did you manage to get an audience with the authorities? Because I sure as hell didn't!" Damion laughed, hoping to keep Ramskill at ease, and talking.

"Not really—I guess I kind of gathered because after the first week it hit the wires, the story was gone. I didn't hear anything more about it . . . "

Not the answer Dellinger wanted to hear. "What do you think, Professor? Did Sanderson have any medical issues?"

"Not that I know of—but, we were colleagues and that was it. When we were young, we hung out together, but after that? Not so much . . ."

"Did he ever tell you about the work he was doing in the Yucatan? At the Great Pyramid?"

"No more than he told the public. All two of them who might be interested . . ."

"I can well imagine it's a pretty specific interest," Damion chuckled. "From what I gather, he was interested in proving a connection between the Mayan culture, and Georgia . . ."

"Well, that's true—however, he kept his research pretty guarded. One thing I know about Richard Sanderson—he kept ninety-nine percent of what he discovered to himself and, most likely, under lock and key."

"I imagine he had quite the safe-deposit box . . ." It was a comment meant to be lighthearted, but Ramskill interpreted it otherwise.

"Richard? Oh, no—he kept everything he had in a safe."

"Seriously? In his house?"

Ramskill nodded. "I can attest to it—the one time I was there, it caught my eye. I asked him about it, and he said he was more comfortable having the artifacts with him." He paused. "At first, I thought it was a little wacky, but, for some reason, it seemed to fit him—so, who was I to say anything?" Another pause. "But, if you ask me? It probably wasn't too tough to steal . . ."

And, there it was—the moment when David Ramskill tipped his hand. *There was no mention of a stolen safe*, Damion thought as he listened intently. "I imagine you're right about that . . ." Suddenly, he offered his hand. "I think that's all—thanks again for taking the time. I really appreciate the information . . ."

With that, he strode out the door, making a mental note.

Tail Ramskill . . .

Peyton Maxwell watched as Damion left Ramskill's office, making it appear as if she were heading toward the stairs. Of course, she had no idea who he was, but, from the timbre of their conversation?

He was someone she didn't want to know.

Moments later, she stood in Ramskill's doorway. "Hello, David . . ." She hesitated, making sure they were alone. "I couldn't help but overhear your conversation . . ."

He eyed her, signaling his disdain. "Yes—he asked for an appointment, and I thought it foolish to decline."

"Who is he?"

"Detective Damion Dellinger—and, as you might have guessed, one of Savannah's finest."

Peyton said nothing, waiting for him to continue.

"He's legit. I checked . . ."

"From what I gathered, he was asking about Richard . . ."

"Yes—but, I didn't give him anything worthwhile. Only what can be verified by a third-rate Internet search . . ."

In that instant, Peyton Maxwell began to put two and two together. "Someone contacted me about Richard . . ."

"What? Who?"

"Colbie Colleen . . ."

"Why was she asking about Richard? And, who the hell is she, anyway?" His voiced pitched up slightly as the vein in his neck began to pulse.

"She's an investigator—a psychic investigator, and she's legit. I checked . . ."

The sarcasm didn't go unnoticed.

Ramskill said nothing, thinking of how such new developments placed them in a precarious position. Finally, he looked at Peyton. "We must be careful . . ."

"So? What do you think?" Colbie took off her glasses, then rubbed her eyes.

"He knows a lot more than he's saying . . ."

"Why do you think so?"

"Because I already knew everything he told me just from basic research—it were as if he were stringing me along, providing just enough information."

"I know the type—and, I'll bet the info he gave you was milk toast."

"Meaning?"

"He gave you information designed to dissuade your interest—it was bland."

"I agree—but, I didn't want to press him to the point of being uncomfortable. It was better to let him think he gave me everything I needed."

"I would have done the same . . ." Colbie paused. "Was he alone when you got there?"

"Yes . . . why?"

"I'm getting a feeling someone else was there . . ."

"Nope—just me. In fact, the place was deserted because of summer break . . ."

"Interesting . . ."

"There was someone heading down the stairs when I was leaving, but she didn't pay any attention to me."

"She? What did she look like?"

Damion took a second, trying to recall. "I didn't see her face, but I remember she had blonde hair . . ."

"Long?"

"I don't know—she had it clipped up. So, it was at least long enough to do that . . . "

Colbie slipped on her glasses, then flipped through her notes. "How old?"

"Thirties, maybe—she could have been younger, or older. Like I said, I didn't see her face—but, judging from her athletic body build, that's probably close."

"Hold on a sec . . ." With a few keystrokes, she uploaded a file, and clicked. "A pic's coming your way . . ."

"Confirmed—just got it."

Colbie waited as he opened the file. "Is that who you saw?"

Damion scrutinized everything about the young woman in the photo. "Could be—I can't be one hundred percent sure. But, just judging by the color of hair, it's definitely possible." He paused. "Who is she?"

"Peyton Maxwell . . ."

"What does she have to do with Ramskill?"

"Maybe nothing—but, I suspect something."

"Did she mention him when you met with her?"

Again, Colbie flipped through her notes to reinforce her memory. "Oh, yes—but, she didn't speak highly of him. In fact, she said he gives her the creeps . . ."

"Then, I doubt seriously she was in the building to see Ramskill . . ."

"You're probably right. But, there's something bugging me, and I'm not sure what it is . . ."

Although Detective Dellinger worked with Colbie during her case in Savannah a couple of years prior, he didn't have an opportunity to see her in action—and, he was impressed. "I'm not too up on how you do things—but, if you think there's something else to consider, I'm game."

"I appreciate it," Colbie laughed. "I'm sure how I approach a case is very different . . ."

"It is—but, you know I have an open mind." He paused, thinking about their investigation. "Where do you want to go from here?"

"Well . . . Peyton Maxwell mentioned someone who's joined at the hip with Ramskill. I think it's time I give him some of my valuable time . . ."

Damion chuckled, enjoying her sense of humor. "Name?"

"Moss. Nathan Moss . . ."

Weeks passed with little to show for Colbie's and Detective Dellinger's efforts—even so, both knew their investigation would ramp up when the university was back in session. As soon as it did?

Colbie didn't waste a second getting to the archaeology department.

After considerable discussion, she and Damion agreed it would be better for her to ferret out information since no one would recognize her. "That's if Peyton Maxwell isn't around," she commented as they discussed the trajectory of their investigation.

"She doesn't work there, does she?"

"No—but, I can't shake the feeling she knows more than she told me a few weeks ago."

"I know this will sound like a stupid question—but, can you tune in before you go to see if she's there?"

"That's not stupid, at all—sometimes, I can. It depends on how strong her energy is—if I feel it when I walk in the archeo department, I'll go to plan B."

"Which is?"

"I'm not sure, but I'll think of something . . ."

After another twenty minutes of discussing the investigation's direction, they clicked off with a promise to keep in touch.

For a good ten minutes after their conversation, Damion sat in his den, thinking. Since the suggestion for his taking a sabbatical arose and was, subsequently, implemented, he questioned whether staying in law enforcement were the direction he wanted to go. Although he questioned it at the beginning of his leave, he soon found he enjoyed working on his own with no one to answer to except himself. *Maybe*, he thought, *twenty-three years on the force is enough . . .*

As he considered possibilities, his thoughts slowly turned to what instigated his sabbatical—what led to mental fracturing to the point his superior requested he take time off. It was something Colbie knew nothing about and, if he were to be honest with her simply out of respect for their working relationship, she should know.

A slow escalation of his inability to handle emotionally taxing aspects of his job began to surface shortly after Colbie wrapped up her case in Savannah, a couple of years prior. At first, signals were veiled, not surfacing full force until shortly before his trip to the Mayan ruins. When they did?

It wasn't pretty.

Mental evaluations were necessary, of course, and there was considerable discussion among his superiors regarding his continued suitability for the force. Still, Dellinger's stellar record and tenure dictated they provide him every opportunity to get his shit together. Ultimately, they came to an agreement—perhaps, all he needed was a little R 'n R.

For a while, it seemed they were right—maybe a few weeks touring the Mayan ruins was exactly what he needed, and he enjoyed having time to himself. Since his divorce nearly a decade ago, there was little free time, his belief being the more he kept busy, the more his heart wouldn't ache. It worked, too—until it didn't.

When home met work?

An emotional Molotov cocktail.

So, when he ran into Colbie Colleen at the Great Pyramid during a difficult time, it was probably the best thing for him. A new perspective is always a good thing and, after working the first twenty-four hours as a freelance investigator, he began to reassess. Was he still cut out for the stress? Maybe. Did he want to deal with it?

Negative.

Chapter 8

Experience does one thing—it prevents one from looking like a complete moron. At least, that's how it usually goes. For Nathan Moss?

Not so much.

As you might suspect, he wasn't one to foster lasting relationships with—well, anyone, really—but, especially those with whom he worked. There were a few exceptions, of course, and working with David Ramskill was one of the best gigs he managed to snag about five years out of grad school. Moss firmly believed linking up with Ramskill was a 'right time, right place' thing, and certainly serendipitous—yet, beneficial to both of them.

David, however, had a slightly different take.

The young man, although a genius, was painfully inadequate when it came to social skills—perfect for what Ramskill dreamed about for years. Moss's ability to blend into the woodwork was a definite plus, and that's exactly what David Ramskill needed—someone malleable. Shy.

Inconsequential.

Sending him to the Maya dig was a stroke of genius, and all it took was a quick call to Richard Sanderson from Ramskill to make it happen. Professor Sanderson, however, wasn't in the habit of meeting those with whom he'd have little contact—so, when Nathan Moss arrived to report for duty, one of Sanderson's assistants met him. The truth?

Richard Sanderson wouldn't have recognized Nathan Moss if he were standing in front of him.

And, David Ramskill knew it.

Nathan's tenure at the dig was something even he didn't expect—a few years in, he was still employed doing something he loved, somehow managing to not get canned. Even so, when the day's work was done, he retreated to his small, one-room cabin, keeping to himself until the following morning. It was a routine that worked well, freeing him from the stress of having to fit his round body into a square hole.

But, when Professor Richard Sanderson was found with his eyes pecked out and his body in a decaying, deplorable state, things changed. Perhaps most alarming was David Ramskill's showing up on a regular basis, pumping Moss for information about the dig—what did they find? Where? Who discovered whatever it was they found?

Relentless in his pursuit of what he wanted, Ramskill ultimately wound up leaving Moss with a choice—either give him what he needed, or kiss the archaeological dig goodbye.

Being the spineless genius he was, Moss immediately opted for working with David Ramskill on a different level— one requiring a modicum of cunning, and stealth. So, it was shortly after Sanderson died, Ramskill tasked Nathan with breaking and entering. "It's a quick get in, get out job," he reassured him. "No one will ever know you were there. Just get the safe, and get the hell out . . ."

Even after tepid assurances everything would be fine, plus a substantial payout, Moss still wasn't convinced— besides, how the hell was he going to carry out a safe? Unless, of course, it was one like his little brother had when he was ten.

But, he didn't think so.

Clearly, there was much at stake and, when Nathan returned without accomplishing his task, he knew to start packing—but, as disappointing as it was to say goodbye to the dig, he left in a position of leverage. You see, one thing David Ramskill didn't know about Nathan Moss—he wrote things down. A lot of things.

Everything.

And, it was upon his return to the States, he decided to put that leverage to use. Certainly, there would be someone who would pay for the information he held . . .

Wouldn't there?

CHAPTER 9

The first thing David Ramskill did after learning about Colbie Colleen's conversation with Peyton Maxwell was a quick search on the Internet. Doing so proved worthwhile—when she waltzed into his office on a warm, fall day, at least he wasn't blindsided.

"Professor Ramskill?" Smiling, Colbie offered a friendly handshake. "I'm Colbie Colleen—do you have a minute?"

"No, not really—I'm sorry. I'm on my way to class . . ."

In that instant, Colbie knew he had no interest in speaking with her. Ever. "I only need a minute—I'll really appreciate it."

Ramskill sighed, loudly enough for Colbie to hear. "You have five minutes . . ."

"Perfect! That's all I need!"

"What can I do for you, Ms. Colleen?"

"Well, I'm investigating Professor Richard Sanderson's mysterious death, and I know he was your colleague . . ."

Ramskill grabbed his briefcase. "I have no idea what happened to Richard." He paused. "Now, if you'll excuse me?"

Colbie didn't budge. "What do you know about the statue, Professor?"

"What statue?"

"The one Richard Sanderson discovered." She paused, cataloguing every twitch and blink as Ramskill decided how he should answer. "Certainly, you're familiar . . ."

Then, he smiled. "Oh, yes—Richard showed it to me shortly after he uncovered it. In fact, I'm one of the few who knew of its existence until the press caught wind . . ." He checked his watch. "I really must go . . ."

"Certainly—I'll walk with you."

Just what David Ramskill didn't want to hear. "My summer class is across campus . . ."

"Oh, I don't mind . . ." Again, Colbie kept an assessing eye on him, knowing he was irritated, yet refusing to show it.

"Really, Ms. Colleen—perhaps another time." With that he brushed by her without so much as a dismissive goodbye.

She watched as he disappeared down the stairs and through the door, knowing he just skyrocketed to the top of her suspect list. *You told me what I needed to know,* she thought as she followed at what she thought was a safe distance—until, suddenly, he turned, glaring at her, then went on his way.

Minutes later, Colbie returned to her car, then tapped a message to Damion suggesting they meet. When he suggested dinner, she gladly accepted, knowing they'd talk business for most of the evening.

Still, dinner will be nice . . .

"Dessert?"

"Oh, no—I'm stuffed!" She watched him drain his water glass. "But, I will have coffee . . ."

"Two coffees comin' up!" He signaled their server and, minutes later, she returned, two bistro-style cups in hand. "I haven't had an evening coffee since I left the force . . ."

"Left? I thought you were on sabbatical . . ."

"I was—am." In that moment, Damion knew he needed to tell Colbie the truth. "But, I'm considering making it permanent . . ."

"What? Why?"

"It's a long story . . ."

And, long it was—for the next hour they sat, Damion confiding his difficulties with depression, and a few other things going along with it. "So—I'm thinking maybe it's time for a change . . ."

"I know how you feel—I was in the Yucatan for almost the same reason. Something just seems to be missing, yet I can't quite figure out what it is . . ."

"Did you reach a point when you felt you weren't doing your best work?"

Colbie nodded. "Yes—and, I began doubting my ability to solve a case, let alone use my intuitive abilities." She paused, thinking how she changed over the past few years. "So, that's when I decided to make a change . . ."

"Did you?"

"Make a change?"

"Yeah—did you have the guts to turn your life in a different direction?"

"Well . . ."

Damion added a little more cream to his coffee. "I don't mean to sound rude, but I know what you're going through. It's not easy—and, I found I had to answer some really tough questions."

Colbie said nothing as she focused on everything he was saying—it was a bit unsettling to recognize herself in his words. Finally, she admitted what she knew to be true. "I'm still at a crossroads—like you said at dinner after we met at the ruins—and, it makes me wonder if I even know what my authentic self is . . ."

"Ah—'authentic self.' The buzz phrase seeming to have caught on over the last few years—the way I see it? It's nothing more than 'what you see is what you get.' If you're not honest with yourself, it's probably hard to be honest with other people—family, friends, or anyone else."

"That's a rather jaded viewpoint . . ."

"Maybe—but, think about it. Authenticity, I think, means being truthful about yourself, as well as to yourself. If you can't be truthful with yourself, then how can you be truthful with anyone?"

"I agree—but, for most people, that's easier said than done. Including me, I guess . . ."

Damion sat back in his seat, looking at her. "Do you want to know your authentic self?"

"Well . . . yes."

"I ask because I found I was much more comfortable going along as I was—which led to depression, anxiety, and just about anything else you can think of, including high blood pressure." He paused, trying to assess Colbie's reaction. "And, to be honest, I think you're afraid of meeting your true self . . ."

Colbie laughed, then took the last sip of coffee. "You sound like a shrink! Is there something you're not telling me?"

Damion met her comment with a good-natured grin. "I guess I do!" A pause. "But, in all seriousness, I want you to be happy—and, I don't think you are."

Colbie nodded. "You're right . . ."

"So—what are you going to do about it?"

"I'm not sure—but, one thing I'm learning while working on this case is to be open to all things. Not just the things that are obvious . . ."

"Or, what you think is obvious . . ."

"True—one thing I noticed over the last couple of years is I began to doubt my ability in nearly everything I did."

"In what way?"

"Oh, mostly with work, I guess—I was quick to judge without thinking of adjacent possibilities. Doors of opportunity would open and close without my taking appropriate notice . . ."

"Sounds familiar—I became a little too cemented in my usual way of investigating. And, it didn't help as much as I figured it would . . ."

So, there they were, trying to figure each other out while trying to understand themselves. Finally, Damion checked his watch. "As much as I enjoy your company, Ms. Colleen, I need my beauty sleep—what do you say we table this conversation for another time?"

"Fine with me!" Colbie tried to laugh off the seriousness of their time together, but it came across as slightly disingenuous—all she could do was hope he didn't notice. But, the truth?

Such introspection was making her nervous.

"I just received the autopsy results . . ."

"And?"

"There's no doubt—Richard was murdered."

Colbie listened as Emma sniffled, trying to collect her thoughts. "Do they know how?"

"Well, there was significant damage to his heart—before today, they weren't sure if it were due to animals because they didn't know how long he was dead before they found him."

"What do they think now?"

"Stabbed in the heart from underneath the ribcage . . ."

"Do they have any idea by what?"

"I didn't ask—I couldn't believe what I was hearing and, after I hung up, I called you . . ."

Fifteen minutes later Emma ended the call, her voice choked with emotion. Of course, the autopsy results tracked with Colbie's interpretation of her vision when she experienced Sanderson's perspective while being chased in the jungle, running for his life.

There's no doubt it was murder, she thought.

No doubt, at all . . .

Nathan glared at Clifford Rasmussen, a newfound resolve in his eyes. "I think my terms are clear, don't you Clifford?"

"Clifford? A little familiar, don't you think? I prefer Dr. Rasmussen . . ."

"Well, luckily, I don't care what you prefer—as of now, you're riding shotgun."

Rasmussen returned his glare. "You seem to forget, Nathan, why you're here. So, in case it slipped your mind, you're to hand over all notes—per our agreement, if you recall. And, you will be paid accordingly . . ."

Nathan Moss didn't avert his eyes, perhaps standing his ground for the first time in his life. "Of course, I recall—but, you and I know agreements are meant to be broken. Surely, what I have to offer is worth much more than previously agreed upon . . . "

"A deal is a deal, Nathan—I don't take kindly to changing parameters based on your unilateral decision." Rasmussen stood, headed for his office door, then gestured to Moss their meeting was over. "It's unfortunate—I hoped we could work together amicably. But, clearly, that's not to be . . ."

Nathan Moss stood, false bravado tanking with each passing second. It never occurred to him Clifford Rasmussen wouldn't agree to his new terms, and leaving without a briefcase full of cash wasn't exactly what Moss had in mind.

"I suggest," Rasmussen continued, his tone direct and unyielding, "you take this opportunity to give considerable thought to your position. If you come to your senses, I will, of course, listen . . ."

With that, Nathan Moss was unceremoniously excused. It was an embarrassment rocking him to his core and, in that moment, he made a promise to himself—give the greedy and insufferable Clifford Rasmussen what he wanted?

Over my dead body . . .

CHAPTER 10

Tabashi Abnal read the short article on Richard Sanderson's mysterious murder, shaking his head. *They have nothing,* he thought, placing his laptop on the handcrafted, wooden stool in front of him. It was one of the few pieces of furniture he had, doing double duty as a coffee table, as well as a place to take a load off. *They're nothing, but ignorant fools . . .*

Sitting on the porch of his small apartment, he adjusted the woven, cane chair so he could watch the sun set behind treetops on the horizon. The long and short of it was he hadn't given Richard Sanderson much consideration since his critter-ravaged body was discovered a few months prior. What truly happened to him he didn't know—but, if he were a bettin' man?

David Ramskill was in deep.

In his mind, there was no doubt—Ramskill was a pain in the ass ever since he met him, and there was no reason to think he changed over the course of the couple of years since they last spoke. Always touting his own self-worth, the Indiana Jones wannabe clearly wasn't aware of his own inadequacies. Or, perhaps he was, yet didn't view them as such—either way, his level of elevated self-importance was nothing less than excessively irritating.

So, when Tabashi saw Ramskill snooping around Sanderson's cabin shortly after his untimely demise?

He knew he was up to no good.

He watched, listening as David rooted around, muttering to himself all the while. It seemed his sidekick—whoever that was—wasn't pulling his weight, and the professor wasn't happy about it Not one bit. At one point, the words 'incompetent asshole' wafted from the tiny, open window, leaving Abnal to wonder, of course, what was so important. Knowing Ramskill as he did, there was the definite possibility his ranting was for no particular reason. That time?

There was more to it.

As sure as he was sitting there on that stiflingly humid summer evening in the Yucatan jungle, Tabashi Abnal knew he witnessed something he shouldn't have.

The question was who should he tell.

It's always interesting when someone changes—you know, an about face when no one's looking. Most who are astute enough to notice, do so with a degree of admiration—until they begin to wonder why. Private conversations at social gatherings turn from pleasantries to something more sinister as if bubbling up from a unknown cauldron. Possible reasons and situations are bandied about, some with an accompanying smile—others, not so much. It was a spot no one cared to be in at a family gathering, or with friends—so when Nathan Moss appeared at the tavern where professors and their ilk met for an occasional drink . . . well, let's just say it sparked conversation.

It was more of a metamorphosis, really—for someone who usually exhibited the confidence of a gnat, sudden bravado was certainly a reasonable topic of barroom gossip. False or not, Nathan's transformation was a mesmerizing shift from someone who lived his life in the woodwork to one who, perhaps, knew a bit too much. Still, it was clear Moss enjoyed his newly-crafted personality, and he seemed to be taking to it like the duck to water thing.

People noticed.

Including Clifford Rasmussen.

Although Rasmussen carried no animosity toward Moss, it was clear their previous working relationship was fractured beyond repair. And, as you can imagine, Clifford didn't think much of Nathan's play for power. But, there was one thing of which he was sure . . .

He had to get his hands on Moss's notes.

Knowing he was one of few who knew of the young archaeologist's propensity for putting his observations of life to paper placed Rasmussen in a leveraged position. There were plenty of people, he surmised, who would love to know what Nathan's journals held, and it wasn't beyond Clifford to use them to his advantage. *Surely,* he thought as he recalled Moss's unsuccessful bid for power, *he must realize the dangers of writing down such things . . .*

It was certainly worth checking out.

Colbie glanced at Damion, then back at her computer screen. "There's something we're missing—there has to be someone else involved. Or, at least, someone who knows something."

"It's a nice thought, but who? We talked to everyone on our list . . ."

"That's my point! We talked to a grand total of three people, if you include Emma . . ."

"Ramskill, and Peyton Maxwell . . ."

"Yes—but, doesn't it strike you as odd there are only two people outside of family who know anything about Richard Sanderson?" Colbie paused, knowing her frustration was beginning to show. "Or, the statue—or, anything else he discovered. I don't know—it just seems like everything Sanderson dried up."

Damion was quiet, thinking. "You're right—for someone of his relative fame."

"At least within the archaeo community . . ."

He nodded. "It stands to reason there are other names involved." Another pause. "What was the name of the grad student Peyton Maxwell mentioned?"

"Nathan Moss . . ."

"Hmm—what do you say we team up?"

"You mean both of us pay a visit to Moss?"

"Well—why not? From what I remember of your conversation with Peyton, Moss is somewhat . . ."

"Pathetic. That's what she said . . ."

"So, if that's the case, maybe both of us ganging up on him will break his already weak resolve . . ."

"It doesn't hurt to give it a shot . . ."

Tacking on another thirty minutes to their already hour-long conversation, both were ready to call it a night. "One last thing," Colbie commented. "Ambush, or plan?"

Damion laughed. "Ambush . . ."

As it turned out, finding Nathan Moss wasn't too tricky—even lowly freshman in the archaeo department knew who he was. "He's always around here," several told them as they headed for class. "Check Ramskill's office . . ."

Of course, that was exactly what neither Damion nor Colbie wanted to do—the last thing they needed was implanting suspicion in Ramskill's mind. But, when they dissected such a conversation's ramifications, Moss's blabbing to his mentor was a good bet. The bottom line?

David Ramskill would know about it.

However, what Colbie and Damion didn't know at the time of planning their surprise visit was Nathan Moss was a new man. No longer did he take crap from anyone—unless they physically threatened him, of course. Anything else?

He was no one's whippin' post.

With little luck finding him outside the university, Colbie and Damion decided to take a shot at locating him in Ramskill's office. "Let's hope," Damion commented as they climbed the stairs to the third floor, "his mentor is nowhere to be found."

Colbie nodded as she sidestepped a wad of gum. "I checked—Ramskill will be in class for the next two hours."

"Good thinking . . ."

Just then, Colbie stopped. "Check it out—Ramskill's door is wide open . . ."

"Excellent—someone's in there even if it's not Moss." He stopped just short of the door, but out of earshot of anyone in the office. "Good cop, bad cop?"

"Are you serious?"

"Well . . . yeah."

"No—no matter who's in there, we don't want to come on too strong." Colbie paused, tapping into her intuition. "I think it's Moss . . ."

Seconds later, they stepped across the threshold, her intuition correct. "Hi," she greeted him, as she approached. "Are you Nathan Moss?"

Moss glared at her, Colbie uncertain if that's the way he was all the time, or she happened to get lucky on that particular day. "Who wants to know?"

She smiled, gesturing to Dellinger. "This is Damion, and I'm Colbie . . ."

At that moment, Colbie realized—felt—Nathan Moss was a duplicitous young man, most likely to gain favor with those who were of a nefarious nature. Not purposely, perhaps—but, it seemed to be where he always landed. "And, you are," Colbie asked when Moss didn't extend the courtesy.

"What can I do for you?"

Damion decided not to dwell on his name. "Well, that depends—if you're Nathan Moss, we'd like to talk to you." It was then the Savannah detective knew taking the soft approach with Mr. Moss wasn't going to work.

He turned to Colbie. "I think he's Moss, don't you?"

Colbie nodded. "He fits the description . . ."

Well, that did it. Moss's shoulders sagged at the thought of being confronted about anything. "I'm Nathan Moss," he finally admitted.

Damion smiled, extending his hand. "Excellent—now that we know each other, we'd like to talk to you if you have a second . . ."

"About?"

"Richard Sanderson . . ."

Moss's stomach lurched. "What about him?"

"Did you know him well," Colbie asked. "When your name came up in our search, it was clear your credentials are topnotch. It only made sense you would know those within the archaeo sector pretty well . . ."

"Well, not really. I heard of him, naturally, but I really didn't have much to do with him, even when I was on his dig."

"You were on his dig?" She glanced at Damion, then returned her attention to Moss. "I think that would be fascinating . . ."

Unfortunately, her attempt at casual conversation fell flat. "It was . . ."

"So, did you meet Sanderson while you were there?"

Nathan nodded. "A couple of times . . ."

Damion's turn. "What was he like?"

"Like any other archaeologist, I guess . . ."

With his answer, it was clear Nathan Moss wasn't too hip on providing any information other than a direct answer to a direct question. "Did you ever have the opportunity to work along side him?"

Moss shook his head. "Nope . . ."

It was at that point Damion ran out of patience. "Did you ever have the opportunity to see the Mayan statue Professor Sanderson discovered?"

"No—it was pretty well known he kept it under lock and key."

"How do you know?"

"Everybody knew—there were only a couple of times he took it out of the safe." It was then Nathan Moss knew he said too much.

"Did you ever see the safe?"

"No—I just heard about it."

Dellinger wasn't about to let up. "Who told you?"

Moss swallowed hard, deciding to clam up. "I think our conversation is over . . ."

With little else to say, Colbie and Damion thanked him, then left, both considering what they just heard. "So, what do you think," Colbie asked as they got in the car.

"Well—my gut tells me he knows a whole lot more than he's saying."

"Mine, too—I think he realized if he answered your question about who told him about the safe, he'd be coughing up information that could get him in a bunch of trouble."

Dellinger turned to look at her before pressing the ignition. "I think, however, Peyton Maxwell's assessment of him was pretty accurate—he doesn't strike me as the tough guy type who would have the stomach for some sort of grade-B espionage."

"Espionage?"

"Like I said, grade B—I think he's a spineless little worm who will do whatever anyone tells him." He paused. "So, it makes me wonder what he was willing to do when he was working at Sanderson's dig . . ."

"Agreed—I also find it interesting he somehow managed to get a gig at a well-known archaeological site. Holy shit—there are people with better credentials than his who get turned away."

"That tells me he had some sort of connection . . ."

She nodded. "And, since he was in David Ramskill's office, it doesn't seem too difficult to figure out . . ."

By the time Detective Dellinger dropped Colbie at her door, both were in agreement. Even though they barely had enough people to consider as some sort of suspect, one thing was clear . . .

David Ramskill was their best bet.

CHAPTER 11

*A*s is often the case in an investigation, when the time comes to fan out in an effort to expand possible sources, one runs the risk of diluting the initial cause. And, yes—while there are merits for doing so, stepping outside the bounds of an original investigation sometimes muddies the water.

"I think we need to talk to other archaeologists at the Yucatan dig," Colbie suggested. "It occurred to me we haven't taken the opportunity to speak to anyone who was there . . ."

"Don't forget Nathan Moss . . ."

"Well, yes—but, I'm talking about the guys who were running the show. I'd be surprised if they didn't have at least one or two who are fairly local . . ."

Damion held the door for her at a local tap, both grateful to take refuge from a stinging, frigid rain. "You're right—we took off before we had any idea of what was going on."

Within minutes, they were enjoying a cozy table for two in front of a massive fireplace. "This reminds me of a ski lodge," Colbie commented, scanning the room. "Somehow, it doesn't quite fit when I think of Georgia . . ."

"True—but, you have to admit it's comfortable." He glanced at her, noticing the firelight flickering on her face. "You look at home here . . ."

Colbie nodded. "I am—I was raised in the northwest. We're all about cozy, and warm . . ."

After signaling the server and placing their order, both were reluctant to resume talking business—even so, they had to make the best use of their time together. "I think we need to head to the Yucatan . . ."

Damion didn't look at her as he dipped a bread stick in soft butter. "Both of us?"

"Well—actually, now that I think about it, there's no reason for both of us to go." She paused. "How about if you go, and I'll stay here to see what I can learn about Nathan Moss, and David Ramskill . . ."

"I don't suppose you have any names . . ."

Colbie grinned, then reached into her messenger bag, extracting a torn piece of paper. "I was thinking about this earlier today, so I gave Emma a quick call to see if she knew who worked with her brother . . . "

"And?"

"Tabashi Abnal . . ." She handed him the paper. "Sorry it's ripped . . ."

"What do you know about him?"

"Not much, other than what's on the Internet. It seems these guys have similar qualifications and education—and, from what I could tell, he was on par with Sanderson."

"How long did they work together?"

"On the Yucatan dig for a little over three years . . ."

"Did they know each other before that?"

Colbie shook her head. "I don't know—like I said, the articles on the Internet weren't great."

"Okay—but, I'm wondering if it will work just as well to set up a video chat. It won't take nearly as much time—not to mention a whole lot cheaper."

"Well—I don't see any reason why that won't work just as well!"

By the end of dinner, the trajectory of their investigation shifted, ramping up their suspicion that the good Professor Richard Sanderson was taken out by a colleague. "That's the only thing making sense—and, the good news is there's really only a handful of people to investigate."

"True . . ." Damion stood and pulled out Colbie's chair, then helped her with her coat. Minutes later, they stood under the tap's canopy, opening umbrellas. "I'll set up the face-to-face with Abnal—do you want to be in the room, listening, or do you want to take part in the interview?"

"You know—as long as we're clear on the questions we want to ask, I think I'd like to listen. I usually don't have that luxury!"

After a hasty goodbye, Colbie turned left as Damion turned right. Although their manner of carrying out an investigation was as disparate as their opposing directions, both knew they worked well together.

A realization making Colbie more than uncomfortable.

Luckily, setting up a video chat with Sanderson's colleague was easier than anticipated. Within a few days of their plan taking root, Damion stared at his laptop screen, waiting to connect.

Finally, a face. "Mr. Abnal! Thank you for meeting with me!" Damion smiled, memorizing the man's features etched by the strength of the sun. Tanned, leathered, and weathered, he was the epitome of someone who spent time digging for the world's tiniest treasures.

After a minute or two of brief pleasantries, Damion launched his first question. "I'm assuming you knew Richard Sanderson quite well—how long did you work together?"

"Oh, yes—although we weren't close as friends, I'm pleased to say we were close as colleagues." Abnal paused. "I guess probably about five or six years—maybe a little longer."

Damion glanced at Colbie as she took notes from the other side of the room, away from the laptop's lens. "I know this is going to sound a little weird—but, if you were enjoying a beer after work with friends and someone asked you what Richard Sanderson was like, how would you describe him?"

"An interesting question—Richard? A quiet man—his ideas, theories, and possible conspiracies were always well thought out."

"Conspiracies?"

"Well, that's what I call them—his latest was thinking the Mayans emigrated to Georgia." Abnal laughed, recalling his colleagues' opinions of Sanderson's theory. "It didn't gain traction, though . . ."

"What made him think that? As highly regarded as he was, it seems a little strange his idea wasn't taken seriously."

The archaeologist hesitated, as if unsure he should tell Damion what he knew. "Someone sure as hell took him seriously, however . . ."

Damion again glanced at Colbie, then returned his attention to the screen. "Not sure I follow . . ."

Again, Tabashi Abnal took his time to answer. "Shortly after Richard's body was found," he began, "I was passing by his cabin . . ."

"And?"

"There was no question someone was inside . . ."

"You mean one of Sanderson's relatives—or, a friend?"

Abnal shook his head. "Oh, no—and, I have no doubt the guy I saw was looking for something."

Male, Damion thought as he listened. "Did you recognize him?"

"Yes—his name is David Ramskill."

"You're sure?"

"Oh, yes—there was no mistaking him. Besides, I heard him talking—to himself—and, I recognized his voice instantly."

"Are you sure someone else wasn't with him?"

"Yes . . ."

"What did he say?"

Abnal thought for a moment, rewinding what he saw and heard. "I couldn't hear all of it, but, I clearly heard 'incompetent asshole.'"

Another glance at Colbie, Damion considering what Abnal just told him. "And, you're sure no one else was with him . . ."

"One hundred percent—I was intrigued enough, I'm embarrassed to say, I waited in the bushes until he left."

"When he left—did he have anything with him?"

"Not that I could see—if he did, it had to be something he could slip into his pocket. Something fairly small . . ."

"How do you know Ramskill?" An elementary question to be sure, but Detective Dellinger learned at the beginning of his career to ask questions to which he knew—or, suspected—the answer. It certainly made sense Tabashi Abnal and David Ramskill crossed paths because of their chosen professions—but, if there were something else, he wanted to know about it.

"In my profession, Detective—the colleague arena isn't exactly wide, and we get to know each other. But, I imagine you already know that . . ."

"I figured. So, there must be something else . . ."

Abnal nodded. "I saw David Ramskill at certain events throughout the years. But, when he began showing up at the dig . . ."

"The Yucatan dig," Damion interrupted.

"Yes. He was there three or four times—which was odd because he didn't have anything to do with the site."

"Do you know why he was there?"

"No—I never saw him with one of the supervising archaeologists."

"Did you see him with anyone?"

Abnal hesitated, as if trying to focus on someone in particular. "Yes—a younger man. I'm sorry I don't remember his name . . ."

"That's okay!" Damion scribbled a few notes, then returned his attention to Abnal. "The younger man— description?"

"Well—there's not much to remember, really. I saw him a few times at the dig, but that was it. He's rather nondescript—probably about six feet, sandy blond hair . . ."

Half an hour later, Damion clicked off, then sat back in his chair, waiting until Colbie stopped writing. "Holy shit!"

"No kidding! What Abnal just told us catapults Ramskill and Nathan Moss right to the top of our suspect list . . ."

She paused. "And, what he told us about Ramskill's being at Sanderson's cabin? I couldn't believe it!"

"I know—if I had any doubt before talking to Abnal that Sanderson was murdered, I don't now."

"First, we need to figure out why Ramskill was there—and, I think he was looking for a safe."

Damion was quiet, wondering if Richard Sanderson's having a safe made sense. "Why do you think so?"

"Because when I met with Emma, she mentioned it. She also said Richard preferred to keep his artifacts with him . . ."

"And, don't forget Ramskill mentioned the safe when I talked to him—in an off-handed way, though. I don't think he realized what he said . . ."

Colbie thought for a second. "That makes me wonder if Ramskill thinks the safe were stolen . . ."

"Or, maybe Sanderson decided it wasn't safe to keep it there, and he took it elsewhere . . ." The detective focused on Colbie. "What do you feel?"

She didn't answer immediately, thinking about what they learned from Abnal, as well as what they already knew from the beginning of their investigation. "I think . . ." She paused. "I think there's a player we know nothing about . . ."

"Any idea of who?"

She shook her head. "No—but, Ramskill was obviously looking for something he figured would be there. And, from what Emma told me, a safe was the first thing Richard bought when he realized he was going to be in the Yucatan for some time . . ."

"So, it makes sense—if Ramskill were searching for it, he isn't the one to walk off with it. Or, his accomplice . . ."

"Nathan Moss . . ."

"Exactly . . ."

"What do you suggest we do?" Peyton Maxwell glared at the man sitting on the couch. "Well, David?"

Ramskill didn't answer for a second, momentarily wondering if he wanted to continue dealing with her. He questioned from the beginning if she had the guts to carry out their plan, knowing her motivation was based on dirty, sordid revenge. "We do nothing . . ."

"Nothing?"

"Why should we? They're fishing! If they had anything, we'd know it by now—besides, why would they be looking at either one of us?"

"Well, for one thing, I know Colbie Colleen suspects—or, probably knows—Richard and I had a long relationship extending beyond professional."

"So? We don't even know why she and that detective are looking at us . . ."

Peyton stood, exasperation beginning to ooze from every pore. "Because he was murdered, you moron! It doesn't take a genius to figure that out . . ."

Ramskill said nothing, knowing she was right. "Well, if they decide to pay either one of us another visit, we just have to stick to the facts—we know nothing."

She glared at him, then grabbed her purse from a chair by the door. "You better hope they don't come calling," she suggested. "And, just so you know? I don't have any intention of living the rest of my life in prison . . ."

With that she was gone, leaving Ramskill to again wonder if she were worth keeping around. *Maybe not*, he thought as he poured himself a glass of wine.

I'm perfectly capable of going it alone . . .

CHAPTER 12

The approaching holiday was the last thing Clifford Rasmussen needed. It was a time of year he found completely insufferable and, if he heard one more holiday song of cheer, it would too soon for him.

As he sat in his favorite chair watching his wife clear space on the mantle for garland that would, undoubtedly, grace it in the near future, it became infinitely clear there was a shift. Nathan Moss's audacity was particularly disturbing, leaving the impression it was time to be a bit more discerning regarding whom he chose to bring into the fold. Even so, the stark truth was Clifford Rasmussen didn't need anyone other than himself to effect any plan he needed to come to fruition.

A byproduct of unchecked arrogance.

Even so, it felt as if there were something afoot—something he didn't quite understand, yet he was certain David Ramskill was at the center of it.

As usual.

In his mind, Ramskill was nothing but a wannabe, inordinately incapable of achieving a level of success on his own. Such academic infertility was something Rasmussen found uncompromisingly repugnant, instinctively knowing Ramskill was a man to latch onto others' successes like a sycophantic sucker fish attaching to a shark.

Perhaps I should get to know him better, he thought as his wife swiped a dust rag over the mantle top. As distasteful as that idea was, it was a viable method to keep an eye on him. Word had it there were those poking their noses into archaeological business, and it was a situation that simply wouldn't do. Of course, he didn't know the particulars—but, if they were, in fact, investigators as the grapevine advised? It was in his best interest to keep a watchful eye.

Clearly, a conversation was in order.

"I find it curious," Colbie commented, staring at her laptop screen, "there's been very little mention of the statue Richard Sanderson found." Pausing as she adjusted her phone so Damion could hear clearly, she couldn't help thinking about her visions when they first picked up the case. "And, what about the blue paint? It was so clear in my vision, but we haven't heard anything about it . . ."

"Do you ever see things that don't come to fruition?" Damion, too, adjusted his phone because of background noise.

"Yes—but, when something is really pronounced, I know I have to pay particular attention to it. So far? Nothing about paint . . ."

"Or, like you said, the statue . . ."

"The other thing that's bugging me," Colbie commented, "is we know Richard Sanderson was murdered, but we have no idea as to why." A pause. "So, because there's been little said about the statue, it makes me wonder if Sanderson were offed because of it?"

"Because of the statue?"

"Yes—otherwise, I can't think of anything that would be a cause for murder."

Again, Damion switched his cell to the other ear, trying to hear above the din of the grocery store checkout line. "I think you're onto something—let's link up tomorrow morning. Breakfast?"

"Works for me—eight-thirty at the tap?"

Colbie tested her coffee, then added a bit more cream. "So, after we hung up, I did a little research on the blue paint thing . . ."

"And?"

"It's a certain blend of ingredients the Maya used—especially for sacrificial purposes."

Damion put down his coffee, disgust apparent. "Oh, swell—we're going from murder to human sacrifices."

"I know—apparently, ancient Maya painted unlucky tribe members blue, then threw them down a sacred well as human sacrifices. A 'cenote,' I think it was called . . ." Colbie paused, taking a sip of her coffee. "The Maya associated blue with their rain deities and, when they offered sacrifices to the god, Chaak, they painted them blue."

"Why?"

"They believed the sacrifice would send rain to make corn grow." Another sip. "They found blue paint on objects—but, until recently, scientists debated how the Maya created the pigment."

"Ah—so, they used it for multiple things!"

"It appears so—and, the other thing about it?" Colbie caught the server's eye for a coffee refill. "It was a paint that couldn't be reproduced until recently—a bunch of people tried, though, without any luck."

"Technology, I presume . . ."

"That's right—by examining pigment samples under an electron microscope, researchers discovered the signatures of its key ingredients. Up until then, nobody figured out how two, key ingredients fused into an incredibly stable pigment."

"I can't imagine there was much of the original blue paint left to study . . ."

"True—but, there is some. Scientists studied pottery found at the bottom of the cenote at Chichén Itzá. Bones, too, if I recall—male."

"Okay—so there's a relationship to the blue paint in your vision. Do you think that's what it meant?"

"Maybe—or, it could have been water. The Maya believed blue paint represented sacred water . . ."

Damion was quiet for a moment, thinking. "Do you feel," he finally asked, "the blue paint has something to do with the statue?"

Colbie nodded. "That's what I'm thinking . . ."

"Makes sense . . ."

"Especially since I saw both in the same vision—usually, when I see two things together, they're related."

"Okay—let's say we're connecting the blue paint to the statue. Was there blue paint on it?" A pause. "I'm not sure that would make sense since it was used for human sacrifice." Damion accepted the server's offer to refill his cup, thinking about the ancient culture. "It's pretty amazing . . ."

"What is?"

"You know—how they figured out stuff well over two thousand years ago. Think about that—they knew how to bind ingredients in paint that took our present time guys a lifetime to figure out . . ."

Colbie nodded. "In one of the articles I read, one of the most distinctive qualities of Maya Blue is its durable and steadfast color. It barely fades and, sometime after the turn of the nineteenth century—a few years, I think—researchers found a sacred cenote with a fourteen-foot layer of blue residue at the bottom."

"What?"

"Yeah—left over from years of blue-coated sacrifices thrown into the well."

"Swell . . ."

"So," Colbie grinned, "knowing that, I think the blue paint may be important, don't you?" She squinted, peering at him from across the table. "You look a little pale . . ."

"Please forgive me, David—I was harsh the last time we met. In no way did I mean to dismiss your concern about the statue as unimportant. Suffice it to say, it's been a difficult time . . ." Clifford Rasmussen hesitated in an attempt to gauge Ramskill's demeanor. *If he says nothing,* he thought, *convincing sincerity will be in order . . .*

"I certainly didn't expect it, Clifford . . ."

"I know, and I apologize." A pause. "There are times, I'm afraid, all of us take a path from which we cannot return—in this instance, I hope we can . . ."

Ramskill didn't say anything—Rasmussen's apologizing was noteworthy in itself. But, to admit his behavior was unacceptable and coupled with contrition?

David couldn't help wondering.

"So," Clifford continued, "shall we rewind to before our ugly conversation?"

"Indeed—all of us have off days. Consider our friendship rewound . . ."

Friendship? Surely, you can't be that naïve! "Excellent!" Rasmussen hesitated collecting his thoughts. "Now—we were discussing, I believe, the statue's whereabouts . . ."

Ramskill nodded. "Yes—it's a concern it hasn't surfaced."

"I understand—but, David, it never was a point of interest to anyone outside of our field. Perhaps—although, I understand it's a long shot—Richard gave it to someone for safe keeping."

"Maybe—but, both of us know for certain he kept his most treasured belongings in a safe. There were few who knew of it in addition to you and me . . ."

"Even so—we'll probably never know. Unless, of course, the person who has it attempts to sell it at auction . . ."

"Or, the black market . . ."

Rasmussen nodded. "You make an excellent point—there would certainly be more money to make when taking that route." Another pause. "But, again, David—the sad fact is we'll probably never know."

"It's worth far exceeds expectations . . ."

"Especially to those outside of our field . . ."

Both men were quiet, gauging each other's veracity. In Ramskill's mind, such an about-face was uncharacteristic for Clifford, his apology was undoubtedly laced with intention.

Clifford?

He thought the same thing.

Although David didn't say enough to make him think otherwise, even though Clifford Rasmussen didn't know the archaeologist well, he knew him well enough to know Ramskill was like a pit bull with its favorite toy. *If Ramskill wants to know the whereabouts of Sanderson's statue, he won't let go no matter what anyone says . . .*

A thought giving reason for pause.

Peyton Maxwell was in a pickle—and, she had a decision to make. If she were to maintain her current course, gut feeling indicated there was more than a chance she'd end up in a cell block not of her choice. The fact Ramskill hadn't figured out Sanderson was murdered didn't speak well of his mental reasoning capabilities, and that was a concern.

A problem.

The other issue? She was fast beginning not to trust him. Certainly capable of throwing her under the bus to save his own skin wasn't out of the question—rather, it was the probability. When she told Colbie Colleen what she thought of Ramskill, she didn't lie—he made her skin crawl. Still, was that reason enough not to effect revenge on Richard Sanderson for casting her aside without so much as a second thought?

Surely not.

The truth was Peyton always had a bent for the dramatic as evidenced by countless photos of school pageants, musicals, and anything else allowing her to be front and center. Once she was out of high school, however? Well, let's just say she forged a new perspective about life—one requiring princesses and performing days to take a backseat while she figured out how she could make her mark. Although she abhorred the idea of working according to someone else's expectations, leaving the impression of a Barbie-doll airhead wasn't exactly what she had in mind. Still, she was first to admit her looks didn't hurt when securing the best, possible job—considering her age—after obtaining her doctorate in archaeology.

A perfect opportunity to build her reputation and bank account.

That's not to say Ms. Maxwell only viewed life from a position of money—quite the contrary. Pecuniary perks didn't enter into it. Her beauty was enough to amp her success in college and grad school, and many expected the stunning young woman to supercede their expectations. There was little doubt in anyone's mind she would be a success, especially those who had the opportunity to work with her. "Smart, and diligent," they said, several gushing a little too much.

It wasn't until Richard Sanderson waltzed into her life— and, out again—did she entertain the thought of ultimate revenge. Those who eyed their relationship yet kept their mouths shut knew she was capable of something other than what she chose to display. Never completely evident, Peyton left many with questions, her recent behavior answering the call to be someone completely unacceptable. Without Richard in her life, how would she achieve the ultimate pinnacle within the academic community?

When she thought about it—during times of intentional introspection—she wasn't sure if she had what it took to go it alone. Of course, she'd like to think she did, but she wasn't so sure. In fact, it was the sole reason she chose to ripen her relationship with Richard—and, with his being gone, things got a whole lot trickier.

Her thought was if she could, somehow, get ahold of the statue, she could make it work to her advantage—the only reason for hooking up with David Ramskill. Both were seeking the same thing—albeit for divergent reasons—their desires eerily similar with fortune running a close second to only one thing . . .

Fame.

To reach that zenith, there was only one thing standing in her way—well, two, if she counted Ramskill. The other?

Colbie Colleen.

Learning she was brazenly snooping around the archaeo department indicated a less-than-veiled attempt to put those who may have information about Richard Sanderson on notice. Clearly, Colleen and her partner were involved in a serious investigation, one that could lead them in her direction more than once. If Peyton's suspicion came to pass?

They'd be standing on her doorstep.

The only question was when . . .

Nathan Moss sat on the floor, journals representing years of his life spread in front of him. Well, not just his life—the lives of those around him, as well. As he picked up each one, his love for people watching escalated to a level few would consider—or, understand. He knew he was the only one who could lay down his passion via the written word—and, that was okay. He didn't need anyone's approval for anything he did.

Not anymore.

Every person in his life required a separate journal, each looking the same on the outside—it was when pages turned did contents reveal the most intriguing details. It was a habit he developed during his junior year in high school, still going after twenty years. Writing about people's sordid little lives provided an almost indescribable comfort and pleasure—a most gratifying unintended result. A certain, elusive power was born when he began saving his work, and it was then he realized in his hands he held what most people crave and fear.

Leverage.

Lovingly, he picked up the journal on Peyton Maxwell, stroking the cover's soft suede, enjoying its smooth, velvety texture. *If only you knew*, he thought as he untied the slender strap, then opened it to the first page. Reading from the beginning was a good way to stay in touch with how things change in one's life. Not only that, in order to use his writing for maximum purpose, it was always wise to reacquaint himself with the whole story.

Although Ms. Maxwell was never aware, Nathan Moss tracked her movements—professional and personal—since the time she decided to have a sweet dalliance with Richard Sanderson. At the time, Moss's thought was the information might come in handy in the future—although, he wasn't sure how. As he read his first entries, however?

All became clear.

Until that evening, how the beautiful Peyton pursued the professor relentlessly—shamelessly—was relegated to his mind's deep recesses. It was information, however, that could be enormously useful if he were to set his plan in motion. To him, such a display of disrespect for the professor's work was unconscionable—and, although oblique, self-interest was always a constant undercurrent. As far as Moss was concerned, anyone who didn't recognize it was an idiot.

But, it wasn't until David Ramskill entered the picture did things get interesting. Even though Moss regarded covert surveillance sordid, low-class, and pedestrian, he couldn't help himself—and, the several times he kept the binos on Peyton's apartment paid off. Why would David Ramskill be visiting her in the wee hours when Sanderson was out of town was anyone's guess, but it didn't take too much to imagine. Such actions, naturally, piqued his interest, sparking questions of there being trouble in paradise for the unlikely academic couple. *Was David Ramskill waiting in the wings*, he wondered as he refreshed his memory, reading each page carefully and with a scrutinizing eye.

Who had the most to gain from Richard Sanderson's being out of the picture? He had three complete journals on David Ramskill, providing little doubt he was jealous of what life hadn't afforded him. He certainly warranted a closer look when it came to carrying out a cold-blooded murder. Peyton, however?

Not so much.

You're a lot of things, he thought as he gently rewrapped the journal a few hours later, tying its leather cord carefully, protecting the pages.

But, are you a killer?

CHAPTER 13

After considerable research, Colbie finally learned who first examined the Mayan statue Richard Sanderson discovered that day not so many years prior. If anyone could provide the information she needed, Dr. Marian Summerfield was the one.

"Thank you for meeting with me on such short notice," Colbie commented, taking a seat across from the archaeologist scholar at a small table in her office. "I hope you have the information I need . . ."

Dr. Summerfield's smile was warm and genuine. "Well, I'm not sure how much help I can be, but I'll certainly try!" She paused while extracting photographs from a manila folder. "I took them when Richard brought the statue to me to authenticate . . ."

"Authenticate? Surely, he was capable of doing that himself!"

"Oh, yes—but, it's always good to have suspicion's corroborated, don't you think?"

Colbie grinned. "You're right—I have to do the same thing in my line of work!"

"I bet you do—so, why don't you tell me why you need to see me, Ms. Colleen."

Colbie took a moment to take off her coat, then settled in for what could turn out to be a long, intellectual conversation. Providing the backstory was critical and, by the time Colbie finished recounting being in the Yucatan when Richard was found dead, Dr. Summerfield thoroughly understood. "So, if I understand your voicemail message correctly, you're investigating a crime—is that correct?"

"Yes—everything my partner and I uncovered lends itself to that train of thought. That's why I'm wondering about the statue—although my sources weren't the best, I learned there was blue paint on the statue." She didn't take her eyes from the doctor. "Is that right?"

She nodded. "Yes—although, it was a very small amount. On the necklace and loincloth . . ."

"Then, I don't understand—if the blue paint were used for human sacrifice to the rain gods, why was it on a statue?"

"Well, that's a good question—as you probably know, the paint was used for ceremonial sacrifice, as well as adorning warriors. It's elements bonded in such a way, it lasted a long time—exactly what they wanted."

"So, you're saying the paint was nothing but an adornment on the statue? Someone just decided to paint it that color?"

Dr. Summerfield shook her head. "Not quite—you see, there was something special about the statue Richard discovered . . ."

"And, that was . . ."

"The statue, I believe, was a warrior commemorated . . ."

"Not a sacrifice?"

"Exactly. I've only seen a few like it, and I think they signified the same thing . . ."

Colbie was quiet, thinking how pieces were fitting together. "I presume the statue Sanderson found was valuable —is that right?"

Dr. Summerfield nodded. "Oh, yes—quite valuable."

"Did the paint make it more valuable?"

"Good question—let's just say it might be one of the most important Mayan pieces found in decades."

"Are you comfortable giving me a figure?"

The doctor shook her head. "I don't think so—but, I know it's worth is considerable."

"I understand." Colbie paused. "Do you know where the statue is now?"

"Well, I assume Richard had it. Why? Do you think it was stolen?"

Colbie shook her head. "Honestly, I don't know. But, with Richard's murder . . ."

"Murder! Who would do such a thing? Richard was a well-respected man in his field and, as far as I know, he was greatly admired!"

"I don't doubt that—but, it does seem a good recipe for jealousy."

The doctor was silent, not enjoying the possibility of her colleagues—or, colleague—possibly involved in something so horrid. "Is there anything I can do?"

"Other than giving me specific knowledge," Colbie answered with a smile, "I don't think so. But, if I need to contact you again, may I?"

"Of course!"

Ten minutes later, Colbie walked out the door, possibilities swimming in her mind. If Sanderson's find were worth a fortune, it certainly upped the ante when it came to considering greed as a motivating factor. *How many jumped in the cesspool,* she wondered as she headed for her car.

How many, indeed . . .

CHAPTER 14

*W*hispers snaked through the archaeology department only hours after news hit the wires—David Ramskill's body was found stiff as a board in a shallow pond on Josiah Jenson's property the day before New Year's Eve, his face spattered with blue paint. "I was trying out my new ATV," Jenson told authorities. "As soon as I got close, I knew something wasn't right when I saw blue paint all over his face . . ."

Really? Damion popped two pieces of bread in the toaster while listening to the T.V. *What was your first clue?*

The reporter held the microphone as the young farmer recounted finding Ramskill's body. "So, I called the cops right away . . ."

Other than that?

Not much to report.

News of Ramskill's unfortunate demise didn't reach Colbie until she returned to Georgia after the holidays. She and Damion felt it best to take a little downtime, Colbie heading back to Seattle while he spent time with family in Savannah. "This was the last thing I expected to hear," Colbie commented when they logged on for a FaceTime chat shortly after her return. "And, it doesn't make our job any easier . . ."

Damion agreed. "There's no question Sanderson's and Ramskill's murders are the mark of the same person."

"Seriously? It's kind of early to determine anything when it comes to Ramskill . . ."

"Maybe—but, the blue paint?" He paused, thinking. "You had the vision of it and the pond, so it's playing into two murders. That tells me it's someone within the archaeology arena and, as far as I'm concerned, we have several suspects."

"Yes—but, don't forget Ramskill was at the top of our list for murdering Sanderson. Clearly, that may not be the case . . ."

"True." He paused. "Not to change the subject, but there's one more thing . . ."

"Oh, great . . ."

"I'm officially on Ramskill's case . . ."

"What? You're back on the force?"

Damion nodded, not quite sure if she were pleased, or otherwise. "My captain called as soon as the farmer found him . . . "

Colbie was quiet, wondering how his working on the case in an official capacity was going to affect her investigation. "I'm stunned—but, it makes sense. How do you feel about it?"

"I'm not sure—but, I couldn't say no. The department is short staffed, and I know they need help . . ."

Again, Colbie was quiet. "So, your leave of absence is over—I guess the obvious question is how will your working in an official capacity affect our working together?"

"As far as I can tell, it shouldn't—after all, we were sort of working together the first time you were in Savannah. It was okay then, so I don't see any reason for things to change."

That settled, conversation turned to particulars. "I know it's still fresh, but do you know anything," Colbie asked.

"Not really—I headed to the crime scene as soon as I got the call, but he's in the coroner's hands now." A pause. "I know I should have told you the second I found out about Ramskill—but, I didn't want to bother you during your time off."

"I appreciate it—has the coroner told you anything?"

"Not much, other than there weren't discernible wounds, markings, or anything else that will give us a starting point."

"Poison?"

"Maybe—too soon to tell, obviously. But, without any telltale signs . . ."

"What about the blue paint? What did it look like?"

Detective Dellinger took a drink of bottled water, then screwed on the cap. "It was the same color as the Mayan paint in the photographs . . ."

"Do you think the mineral components are the same?"

"Who knows? We won't know that until we get results from the lab . . ."

"What's your gut?"

Damion hesitated, knowing his answer could catapult them to somewhere they hadn't considered. "I think it's the same . . ."

Colbie scratched a few notes, then focused again on the detective. "If that's the case, it narrows down our list of suspects considerably—who knows how many people know about the Mayan blue paint? I'll bet not many . . ."

"Agreed. Anyway—unfortunately, I won't have the time to investigate with you, so I'm afraid that lands in your court. I'll keep you apprised on my end—but, for now, you're kind of on your own. Unless you want to give it up . . ."

"Give it up? Not a chance! I'm a big girl," she laughed. "It's not like I haven't been in this position before—but, I confess it won't be as enjoyable."

Damion said nothing, curious about her comment. "Well—we need to touch base every couple of days unless something major happens. That said, if there's something you need to know, I'll text you immediately . . ."

And, that's where they left it.

As soon as they clicked off, Colbie sat for a second, trying to regroup. Of course, she worked investigations by herself plenty of times, but, for some reason, that time felt different. No longer did she have Brian, Ryan, or Kevin to help her whenever she needed it—and, it was a situation she wasn't sure she liked. For a brief time, Damion took their place—and, although she didn't consider it, she should have known things could change. Would change.

Not necessarily for the better . . .

It wasn't until well into January Colbie learned the lab results. "It's exactly the same mineral makeup as the Mayans," Damion told her during their update session.

"Just as you thought—and, as we discussed, that narrows the field considerably. But, I didn't see anything about his being stabbed . . ."

"Well, you can't see everything, I suppose . . ." Damion teased. "But, you're right about it's narrowing the suspect pool—what's on your agenda for the coming week?"

Colbie thought for a second, knowing she needed to have another conversation with Peyton Maxwell. When Colbie called, however, it was clear the young archaeologist had no intention of gracing her with an audience. "I'll try to talk to Peyton again, but I think she's a closed door . . ."

"Then, she needs to open it—what about surveillance?"

"I'm thinking the same thing—she'll recognize my rental, so I'll turn it in and get something else." She paused, an unsettled feeling beginning to rise. "There's something about her I really don't trust, and it's time to figure it out . . ."

Throughout life, there always comes the time for the necessity to reassess—you know, take personal stock. Colbie did so before deciding to head to the Yucatan, and it wasn't particularly pleasant. To many, it's a journey into the dim recesses of their minds warranting more than a second or two to consider an adjustment. To others?

They could care less.

So, it wasn't until Nathan Moss knocked on Peyton Maxwell's door did she have the opportunity to experience her own version of purposeful introspection. His was a visit she didn't expect, of course, but, when he crossed the threshold to her apartment with three, leather-bound journals in hand, she couldn't help but wonder why.

"I hope I haven't caught you at an inopportune time . . ."

She wanted to tell him that's exactly what it was, but her sense of breeding didn't allow. "How nice to see you, Nathan! Please—come in!" She eyed the journals. "What are those?"

A condescending smile. "These? Just a few things I thought might interest you . . ." Unsuspecting she had no idea her life was about to change, Moss was counting on it.

After expected pleasantries, he placed the three journals on Peyton's glass coffee table, opening the first with a gentle hand. "I think you'll be surprised . . ." He glanced at her. "How about if you do the honors?"

"Me?"

He handed her the first journal. "I think it's fitting . . ."

Slowly, she untied the leather strap. "I can't imagine . . ."

"I bet you can't!" Although she didn't see, a slight sneer crossed his lips.

On the first page was her name written in stunning calligraphy script. "Me?" She glanced at him, her heart beginning to race.

"There's more . . ."

For the next five minutes, Peyton said nothing as she read—then, the explosion he hoped would happen. But, before she could do anything rash, he snatched the remaining two journals from the table, cradling them in his arms as he would beloved schoolbooks. "How dare you!" Her scream was accompanied by the vein in her neck beginning to pulse.

"Me?" He watched as she began to pace, her world of comfort and confidence crumbling. "I'm just giving you a heads up! You can't be so foolish as to think the authorities won't be knocking on your door!"

"My door? What are you talking about?"

Nathan cast a glance that would cause the most stalwart to shrivel. "For someone so intelligent, it pains me you're so dense . . ."

Well, that did it.

Peyton picked up her cell, tapping the screen to life, her fingers trembling. "I'm calling the cops . . ."

Gently, Moss took the phone from her, laying it on the table, then the journal she held in her hand. "There's no need—there's only one reason I'm here."

Peyton swiped at newly forming tears with her fingertips. "I don't understand . . ."

He took her hand—something he wanted to do since the first time he saw her. "Don't worry—I won't show these to anyone . . ."

A sniffle. "But . . ."

Then, Nathan squeezed her hand a little too hard. "You see, Peyton—my love for writing has come in handy over the years." He gestured to the journals, then returned his focus to her. "These are for you—about you. There are more . . ."

"But, I don't understand . . ." She withdrew her hand, the touch of his fingers causing her stomach to churn.

A gesture not unnoticed.

"Of course," he commented, "if you take the time to read all of these . . ." Again, he gestured to the journals, his hands clammy. "You'll see you're in quite a precarious position— one that could land you in a heap of trouble." A steely glare. "But, it doesn't have to be that way . . . "

In that moment, Peyton's patience snapped. She rose, then headed for the door, opening it as she launched a look that would make most men cave. "Get out . . ."

"But, there's more . . ."

"Get out," she screeched again, her voice dripping with contempt.

Her reaction was, naturally, exactly what Moss expected. The beginning pages of the first journal consisted of explicit, prurient, and salacious details regarding her relationship with Sanderson—details, he was certain, she didn't want anyone to know. "I mean you no harm," he commented as he tightened his grip on the leather.

With that, he left, knowing his position was stronger than when he arrived. *Like I always say . . .*

It's all about leverage.

Always a drag when she couldn't put puzzle pieces together, Colbie finally decided the reason she couldn't do so was because she didn't have enough information. Next on her agenda? A chat with the coroner who conducted Richard Sanderson's stateside autopsy. "There's a chance he won't divulge any information," she commented during a quick conversation with Damion.

"I can help things along . . ."

Colbie paused, questioning if she needed it. Then again, why not? "If you can get me in the door, I'll take care of the rest . . ."

"Consider it done—how soon?"

"As quickly as possible—I've been thinking about why nothing seems to be gelling, and talking with the coroner should either confirm my suspicions, or flush them down the drain . . ."

"Care to share?"

"Well, the first thing I want to know is the condition of Sanderson's body when they conducted the autopsy here . . ."

Damion was quiet, thinking there was something she wasn't telling him. "That's it?"

"Well, no . . ."

He waited, instinctively knowing she wasn't going to answer. "Okay—I'll get in touch with the coroner's office to let them know you need a few minutes of their time."

"Perfect . . ."

With that they rang off, each hoping Colbie's discussion with the coroner yielded results. *It's a crapshoot*, she thought as she began to review her notes on Sanderson for the umpteenth time.

Nothing, but a crapshoot . . .

The fact Nathan Moss exhibited such audacity to knock on her door was more than Peyton could fathom. Always thinking of him as a slimy, little worm was more apt than initially thought, and there was no question he must be dealt with accordingly. The fact he had information inflammatory enough to end her archaeology career was concerning—but, with David Ramskill winding up six feet under?

Without doubt, there was another player in the game.

Who, Peyton had no idea, so it certainly seemed prudent to begin winnowing her suspect list to the top three who had reason to want both men dead.

And, why.

The unsettling fact was if there were someone acting against her best interests and she didn't know about it, her position was precarious in more ways than one. Although, at the time, she figured few people knew about her tryst with the professor—unfortunately, an erroneous assumption. She and Sanderson were topics of conversation at more than one bar or dinner table, most of what was discussed fit only for adult ears.

The whole thing reeks, she thought as she laid out a plan to take care of whom she considered a blight on humanity. Of course, it would take time, but there was no question she could right her position within the academic community if she played her hand well. There was no reason she couldn't succeed for there was one thing most people didn't realize coursed through Peyton Maxwell's veins . . .

A mean streak. A mile wide . . .

And, a mile deep.

"Please, have a seat, Ms. Colleen . . ."

Colbie arranged her jacket on the back of a chair, then turned her attention to the county coroner sitting behind his desk. "Thank you for your time—I know you're busy, so I'll get right to the point . . ."

Doctor Irons nodded slightly. "Glad to help—Detective Dellinger told me you need the autopsy results for Richard Sanderson, as well as David Ramskill . . ."

"Yes—I know it's unusual, especially since I'm not directly related to the case."

"Indeed—he explained the circumstances, and I see no harm. I'll make certain the good detective receives a summary of our discussion . . ."

"Excellent—I'll do the same." A brief pause. "So—as you probably know, I'm working with Detective Dellinger on the murders of Richard Sanderson, and David Ramskill."

"How can I help?"

"I'd like to know about the blue paint . . ."

The coroner was quiet, not taking his eyes from the striking redhead. "Please explain . . ."

Colbie shifted in her chair, slightly uncomfortable by the doctor's unyielding attention. "Well, I know from Josiah Jenson's interview with the press there was blue paint on David Ramskill . . ."

"That's correct . . ."

"Was there blue paint on Richard Sanderson, as well?"

And, there it was . . . the million-dollar question no one had the presence of mind to ask until that moment. Few within the ranks of the investigative unit knew, but as far as the public?

Not a word.

"Detective Dellinger didn't discuss this with you?"

She shook her head. "No—but, we've had little time to talk about recently revealed particulars." She paused. "If you're uncomfortable divulging the information, I completely understand . . ."

It was clear the doctor was conflicted, but, simply based on Dellinger's call, he figured telling her about Sanderson couldn't do any harm. "To answer your question, Ms. Colleen, yes—Richard Sanderson did have blue paint on him. But, but very little . . ."

"Much less than David Ramskill?"

Doctor Irons nodded. "Yes—a fraction in comparison."

"Do you happen to have photos of it?"

An usual question—most, outside of police personnel, who had the opportunity to sit in front of his desk weren't the inquisitive types when it came to grisly photos. "I do . . ."

"May I see them?"

Saying nothing further, Dr. Irons buzzed his assistant, requesting the pictures. Moments later, a stocky, fifty-something woman breezed in, handed him a large manila envelope, then blew out again in what seemed like one fluid movement. "My—she's efficient," Colbie commented with a smile.

"Indeed—she's amazing, and I don't know what I'd do without her." Without opening the envelope, he handed it to Colbie. "Fair warning—they're gruesome."

She nodded, appreciating his concern. "As the saying goes, 'it's not my first rodeo . . .'"

He watched as she extracted each photo, scrutinizing them with a critical eye. "Did you test the paint?"

"Test it for what?"

"Well—the main thing is mineral composition. I find it interesting Sanderson was murdered in the Yucatan . . ."

"I'm not sure I follow . . ."

"The paint—the Mayans used a specially formulated blue paint to adorn their sacrifices or warriors." Colbie placed the photos in the envelope, then slid it across the desk. "Doesn't it strike you odd two men—both archaeologists— are murdered with blue paint on them?"

"Yes, it does—but, until this moment, I had no idea the blue paint was significant to the Mayan culture. Or, that it was used as a sacrificial adornment . . ."

"Nor did I until I dug a little deeper . . ." She figured it wasn't the time to tell the good doctor about her vision of blue paint and the Mayan statue—as a man of science, it was a good possibility he would immediately put her in the nutball category. "Through my research, I learned the paint is comprised of certain mineral components allowing it to remain for long periods—but, I'm wondering if there were something else in the paint besides its original components."

"Such as?"

"Well, I'm not sure—I have to wonder, though, if there could have been a fast-acting poison added to the paint." She paused, thinking. "Something that can be absorbed through the skin, or taken by mouth . . ."

"How fast acting?"

Again, Colbie was quiet. "I don't know—immediate?"

"Then, that puts you in the toxicology range of cyanide—possibly hydrogen cyanide."

"Obviously, I've heard of cyanide—but, knowing what I know now, I think any type of poison would be leading the detective and me down the wrong path."

"That's probably wise. Besides, as you can see, David Ramskill was stabbed from just below the rib cage into the heart . . ."

CHAPTER 15

*A*ging. We can only hope we gain a modicum of wisdom by the time we're old enough to know life is rarely as it seems. Always fluctuating in accordance with shifting situations, we often morph into someone others don't recognize—a fact causing great consternation to those secretly praying for a return to the norm. For Peyton Maxwell?

Too much water under the proverbial bridge.

The more she thought about Nathan Moss, the more she knew she must take matters into her own hands. It was an iffy situation, too—up until he was found frozen like a Popsicle, David Ramskill was the one to do their dirty work. Without him?

She was on her own.

So, when Colbie Colleen rapped on her apartment door unannounced, she wasn't quite sure what to do. Quickly, she recovered, however, inviting the investigator in as if she were an old friend. "I didn't think I'd be seeing you again!"

Colbie laughed, offering her most engaging smile. "I bet! Honestly, I wasn't planning on stopping by, but I was in the area . . ." A line of B.S.? Undoubtedly—but, it was also a signal Colbie was familiar with bogus excuses.

"Well, I'm glad you did! What can I do for you?"

Colbie motioned to the dining table. "Do you mind if we sit? I've been on my feet all day!"

It was a request Peyton didn't expect, falsely hoping Colbie would state her business then head for the door. "Of course . . ."

Moments later they were seated across from each other, Peyton refusing to be first to start the conversation. "Well, you know I'm investigating Richard Sanderson's murder," Colbie began. "What can you tell me about David Ramskill's?"

Peyton's eyebrows arched. "David's murder?"

"Yes—doesn't it strike you odd he was spattered with blue paint?"

"Well . . ."

"Paint exactly like that used by the Mayans?" Colbie watched her carefully, mentally cataloguing every move. "I'm sure you heard . . ."

"I did—but, I don't understand why you're asking me."

"Because you had relationships with both men, Peyton—that's obvious." By her tone, Colbie was making it clear she wasn't in the mood for deception.

The archaeologist's face flushed. "I don't know what you're implying, but . . ."

"I'm not implying anything—I'm telling you I know you had relationships with Richard Sanderson, and David Ramskill. That places you directly in the crosshairs . . ."

So much for playing nice.

Peyton's eyes turned dark, narrowing with Colbie's accusation. "You know nothing—and, I have to tell you nothing." She stood, pushing her chair back with her legs. "If you'll excuse me, I have things to do . . ."

Colbie didn't move. "What can you tell me about Nathan Moss?"

Suddenly, Peyton's bravado dissolved, tears welling. "Nathan?"

"Yes—you know exactly who I'm talking about. You called him 'pathetic,' if I recall correctly. It doesn't take a genius to figure out you have little use for him . . ."

Peyton sat, trying to figure out her best position. If she confided in Colbie about Nathan's journals, it would only serve to heighten her suspicions. "I don't. But, I don't understand what Nathan Moss has to do with any of this—do you think he murdered David?"

A classic under-the-bus move.

"I didn't say that—but, considering the relationship you had with Richard, wouldn't you like to know who decided to end his life?"

Another question Peyton wasn't too hip on answering. The truth was her relationship with Richard turned sour—something she refused to discuss with anyone. Odd, too, since it was something crushing her to the point of poor decisions. "Of course," she replied, her voice approaching reverent.

"Then, it's best if you tell me what you know. If you have any involvement, at all . . ."

"You think I had something to do with killing Richard?"

Colbie shook her head. "No . . ."

"David?"

"It crossed my mind . . ."

Well, that did it. "How dare you!" Peyton again stood, every part of her body tensing with anger. "Get out!"

On another day, perhaps, Colbie would have apologized for such brutal honesty. That day?

Peyton's outburst told her everything she needed to know.

Although a linear sort, Nathan Moss—for some inexplicable reason—couldn't quite think clearly enough to formulate the next step of his plan. Thrilled Peyton reacted according to his intent, he was well aware the next one on his list may not be so predictable. *I suppose*, he thought as he leafed through pages of journals four, five, and six, *I can use the same tactics I used on Peyton* . . . but, the moment the ill-gotten idea entered his mind? Nixed. She was the easiest to intimidate—the others?

Not so much.

It was a risk, however. To fully engage the neophyte stages of his plan, he needed time off work—something he didn't have coming for a few months and, in his mind, it was a circumstance ruining everything. Still, Nathan was nothing if not creative, his newly adopted mantra of 'where there's a will, there's a way,' working well when coupled with a false sense of bravado.

A week later?

First class on a jet bound for south of the border.

"Do you think she murdered Ramskill?" Damion poured two glasses of merlot, then placed the bottle to the side.

Colbie paused, thinking about her recent conversation with the beautiful blonde. "You know—I'm not sure. There's something that seems way off, not to mention she appears an obvious suspect."

"True."

"Sometimes, what's right in front of us . . ."

"There's nothing wrong with obvious—and, in this case I agree with you. We have little on Ramskill—the only thing we really know is it has to be someone who knows the significance of the blue paint."

"There's no denying she was trying to deflect my attention to Nathan Moss—and, she was pretty good at it. I thought it interesting she was offended when I implied . . ."

"Or, stated directly . . ."

Colbie laughed. "Well, yes—anyway, when I mentioned I was considering her a suspect for Ramskill's murder, that's when she threw Moss under the bus." She paused, thinking of the connection between Peyton and Nathan. "There's something about Moss she's not telling me . . ."

Damion sat back in the booth, scanning the restaurant as any detective worth his salt would do. "I don't know—if you're thinking she was having some sort of relationship with him, I don't see it."

"No—it's not that. When I talked about him, it were as if she were afraid. Of what, I don't know . . ."

"I can't imagine anyone's being afraid of Moss," he laughed, taking a sip.

"I'm not so sure—what if he has something on her?"

"Such as?"

"Who knows—I did, however, let her know he's on our radar. Just not why . . ."

So, for the next hour they sat, enjoying each other's company. It had been a long time since Detective Dellinger felt so comfortable with someone he barely knew—yes, he knew Colbie from a professional perspective, but, when it came down to it, he knew nothing of her personal life, except the tidbits she dropped as a well-intentioned trail. Even when they were working a case together in Savannah a few years prior, she revealed little when it came to her personal life, something he found refreshing. Then, he had no reason to be curious about things he didn't understand. At that moment?

He wanted to know everything.

Suddenly, Colbie changed the subject. "So—what about you? Is returning to the force the right decision?"

"So far, yes—but, to be honest, nothing's changed. As much as I know I'm needed, my heart really isn't in it . . ."

"Seriously? I figured you'd be glad to be back!"

"Maybe I was—for the first week. After that? Same tension. Same stress. Same everything . . ." Another sip, then he placed the goblet on the table. "I have to say, it wasn't nearly as stressful while we were working the case . . ."

"Well, we still are . . ."

"You know what I mean—working with you, I felt as if I were following my gut. You know, no one to answer to . . ."

As she listened, Colbie recognized doubts she struggled with for the past year. "I know what you mean—but, I guess the question is why."

"Not sure I follow . . ."

Colbie grinned, knowing that was a line of crap. "Oh, please—you know exactly what I mean! You know you want that particular type of freedom, but why do you want it?"

"Ah—Colbie Colleen. Shrink extraordinaire . . ."

"Damned straight!"

Damion chuckled, hoping she didn't see the delight in his eyes—other than his captain from time to time, nobody called him on his B.S. "I don't know . . ."

"Sure you do—just like I did when I decided to take a break to figure out who I really am, and what I want to do." She paused, a softness beginning to fill her heart. "It's nothing to be ashamed of—although, I admit to feeling slightly embarrassed because I was a grown woman acting like a teenager trying to figure out what classes to take . . ."

"It didn't show . . ."

Colbie nodded. "It did to me—and, I couldn't stand that about myself."

"You don't strike me as the type to beat yourself up for not knowing where life would take you . . ."

"But, I am . . ."

Dellinger sighed softly, considering whether to confide—until, finally, a decision. "My wife hated it when I began to question what I was doing, and why I was doing it. She didn't understand . . ."

"In what way?"

Shifting in his seat, he wanted another glass of wine, yet knew he shouldn't. "During the last year of being together, she didn't hesitate to tell me how weak I am . . ."

"Because you wanted to explore other opportunities?"

He nodded. "Sort of—but, then again, she had an unhealthy perspective about a lot of things."

Colbie said nothing, feeling his emotional pain from across the table.

"But, I have to admit, for the last few years of our marriage, I changed . . ."

"And, obviously, she didn't like it . . ."

"That's an understatement—as soon as I mentioned I needed to take a little time off, she was out the door, and on to someone else."

"Swell . . . kids?"

"Grown—barely."

"Well, if there's any bright spot, that's probably it . . ."

Damion nodded, then drained his glass. "At least I know they didn't have to go through the ugliness."

A gentle silence between them, each knew not to press further. "On that note," Colbie finally suggested, "I think it's time to call it a night . . ."

Placing her napkin on the table, she stood, Damion doing the same. "Sorry to be such a downer," he commented, helping her into her coat.

She turned, looking into his eyes. "Sorry? I feel honored you confided . . ."

Minutes later they parted, each unsure of their personal thoughts. Damion watched as Colbie unlocked her car then climbed in, buckling her seat belt before engaging the ignition. Was he interested? Yes. Should he be?

Nope.

The second his feet touched Yucatan soil, Nathan felt as if he were home. It was the one place he felt at ease with himself enough to entertain thoughts of what he was going to do with the rest of his life. Archaeology aside, there was a certain satisfaction when deciding how to alter one's life—just not his own, of course. Doing so was, perhaps, the sole reason for his existence—at least, that's what he thought as he climbed the steps to Richard Sanderson's one-room cabin. *With Ramskill in the ground,* he thought, *at least I can take my time . . .*

He paused, noting the door was opened a crack—a foolish mistake if there were, indeed, secret items to discover. It was something Ramskill would do, but, considering the time passed since Tabashi Abnal spied him rooting through Sanderson's things, it didn't make sense. *Someone else has been here since then . . .*

A surging unease attempted to settle as he pushed gently on the door, allowing it to open just enough to peer inside. What he was expecting, he wasn't quite sure—what he saw, however, wasn't it. The few pieces of furniture Sanderson had were splintered into pieces as if hacked apart with a machete—which, Moss figured, wasn't a stretch considering Sanderson lived in the jungle.

Stepping inside, his tall frame contributed to the uncomfortable, claustrophobic feel—how Sanderson could live there was beyond anything Moss considered tolerable. When he worked on the dig, his living quarters weren't palatial, but they surely beat the hell out of Sanderson's pad.

As he scanned the room, it was clear no one had been there for a while. It made sense, too, though Moss doubted authorities made a concerted effort to determine the particulars of Sanderson's passing. They weren't exactly diligent in their work, sparking little doubt they barely lifted a finger.

Ten minutes later he was out the door, convinced there was nothing to discover—whatever Sanderson was keeping to himself or squirreled away for a time that no longer would come was long gone. Next?

The main act.

Natasha Ramskill sorted through her husband's things, markedly aware the world is made up of those who succeed, those who fail, and those who don't care to try. Her husband?

Master of all three.

Thinking about it, being married to such a man seemed foolish, though it didn't seem so when they skipped town to forever tether themselves to each other's soul. The epitome of tall, dark and handsome, he swept her off her feet, allowing no time to breathe as he continually attempted to convince her he was the one. Was he? Perhaps. But, there was only one thing that mattered to his lovely wife . . .

Bucks. And, a lot of 'em . . .

So, you can imagine what a bitter pill it was when she realized her husband was nothing but a sycophantic hack, destined to always trail in the shadow of . . . well, someone. It was a fact not sitting well and, after more than a decade of marital bliss, Natasha considered calling the whole thing off. David's inability to make it to the top of the academic world stuck in her craw unrelentingly, causing her to barely stand the sight of him whenever he walked through their door.

Which he rarely did.

Of course, authorities interviewed her on several occasions, but there was nothing to tell. "My husband, Detective Dellinger, wasn't a man of means," she offered when he arrived unannounced a few weeks prior.

"What does that have to do with anything," he asked. "All I want to know is if your husband ever mentioned difficulties at work . . ." Hers was a peculiar comment, causing him to wonder if it were a feeble attempt at diverting conversation.

"Well, I only say that because he wasn't the type to need or want things . . ." Her voice turned, suddenly laced with a sneer.

A memory of a conversation she didn't care to keep.

But, my darling, you were certainly a man who needed things . . . Gingerly, she slipped her hand into her husband's favorite pant's pocket, fingertips exploring its recesses, seconds later extracting a key. Her stomach lurched, realizing it was a house key, but not theirs. Turning it in her fingers, an angry flush crept up her neck as she immediately understood its implication.

Of course, she always suspected—too many evenings she sat alone as he claimed work to do at the university. But, that was okay—she preferred her own company to his. Still, as she sat, key in hand, she couldn't help but wonder who turned his eye.

But, none of that mattered—as long as she got her fair share, she could've cared less whether he were at her side, or otherwise.

Keeping emotions buried, she checked the other pocket, curious when her fingers touched a creased piece of paper. "At least it's not another key," she muttered, unfolding it carefully. Definitely her husband's handwriting, she stared at a series of numbers, unsure of their meaning. A phone number? Maybe. The only thing squelching that idea was the digits weren't offset by dashes as they usually were—the way her husband always wrote them.

A code? Another maybe. Or, perhaps the numbers meant nothing—a thought she immediately dismissed. If David Ramskill wrote something down, it was important—usually something he needed to address. Checking the back of the paper before tucking it her jeans, she suddenly knew . . .

A combination . . .

Having worked at the dig for so many years proved an advantage when walking through the site—a few said hello, most nodding their greeting, undoubtedly wondering what the hell Nathan Moss was doing there. But, he didn't care—

they were nothing to him, and the fact was they weren't integral to his reason for visiting.

Approaching the latest discovery location, he caught sight of Tabashi Abnal scrutinizing a relic, then handing it to a freshman archaeologist. As Moss approached, he listened as the senior authority on the dig issued familiar orders, then turned, noticing Nathan coming toward him.

Moss extended his hand. "Mr. Abnal—it's good to see you!" He smiled, clutching three leather journals close to his chest. "It's been a while!'

Tabashi Abnal grinned, although he wasn't particularly pleased to see the man who stood in front of him. "What brings you back?"

"A much needed conversation . . ."

Abnal's eyes narrowed. "With?"

"Well, you, of course!" He patted the journals with his free hand. "I have something in which you may be quite interested . . ."

"A discovery?"

Moss smiled. "Well, yes—of sorts." He waited, and it was becoming increasingly clear the senior archaeologist wasn't greeting him with open arms. "Do you have a few minutes?"

Something telling Abnal to steer clear took a back seat, curiosity tightening its grip. "A few . . ."

Minutes later, they sat at a table in his makeshift office offering a clear view of what was happening at various locations of the dig. "Now—what's your discovery, Nathan? I'm afraid I don't have much time . . ."

Moss nodded. "I understand—so, I'll get right to the point." Untying the leather strap from the first journal, he opened it gently, then slid it across the table. "I think you'll find this interesting reading . . .

Abnal said nothing as he read, his eyes cold when he again turned his attention to Moss. "How did you get this," he asked, his tone dripping contempt.

"That's not important—I think you'll readily agree the information I have is quite damning. Enough to change your circumstances considerably . . ."

"Surely, you're not threatening me . . ."

"Threatening? Of course not—but, you have to agree what I have in that journal as well as these . . ." He patted the two he held on his lap. "Well, let's just say there's more . . ."

Tabashi stood slowly. "If you think I'll be blackmailed, Mr. Moss, you're mistaken . . ."

"Who said anything about blackmail? I simply figured it was prudent to make you aware of circumstances . . ."

"What circumstances?"

"Richard Sanderson, of course—and, David Ramskill."

It was then Tabashi Abnal made a decision—one he considered for quite some time. "Do what you will with your information—it is of no concern to me." He glanced at the changing weather. "It appears it's going to storm, Mr. Moss—for suitable cover, I suggest you take your journals elsewhere."

He waited as Nathan grabbed the opened journal, then stepped from the makeshift tent into what was quickly becoming a torrential downpour. Not bothering to offer a goodbye, he clutched the journals under his shirt, protecting what represented his ultimate hand. Abnal's reaction wasn't what he hoped for, or expected—and, it was one causing him to rethink his plan. *If Abnal reacted that way*, he thought as he darted to the nearest canopied shelter, *what about the others?*

A question he didn't want to entertain . . .

But must.

CHAPTER 16

"She was weird . . ." Damion adjusted the sound on his computer monitor, then turned his direct attention to Colbie. "Nothing like I thought she'd be . . ."

"Weird how?"

"For starters, there wasn't a shred of grief—I got the impression she wasn't too fond of her husband."

"That doesn't surprise me. There was absolutely nothing on the Internet about his being married, so that tells us there may have been trouble in paradise . . ."

"Maybe—but, I think that's a stretch. A lot of people don't want their personal lives plastered on social media, or anywhere else."

"Did she strike you as the private type?"

Damion shook his head. "No—she struck me as the type who likes a good shopping trip."

"Why do you say that?"

"Because their house wasn't anything like I expected— if Ramskill's office were any indication of his decorating preference, he didn't have much input when it came to his home."

"Ritzy?"

"You could say that—although the decor straddled the fence of bad taste."

"Strange . . ." Colbie closed her eyes, tapping into her intuitive mind. "She feels cold."

"What do you mean?"

"You know—unfeeling. There's a lot of negative energy around her . . ."

Damion was quiet, allowing her to access whatever it was she wanted to know.

"There's something about her I definitely don't like. And, until a few weeks ago, she wasn't on our radar . . ."

"Is she now?"

Colbie nodded. "I think so. And, I feel as if she's connected to someone else we've already spoken to . . ."

"Any idea of who?"

"No—but, I also have the distinct feeling one of the main players is someone on the periphery. Someone we may have talked to, but dismissed . . ."

Damion flipped through his most recent notes. "We haven't really cut anyone loose—Maxwell and Moss are still at the top of the list. Ramskill was, but . . ."

Colbie opened her eyes, taking a second to refocus. "You know what really bugs me about this whole thing?"

"What's that?"

"We don't have a reason for any of it! Why was Sanderson murdered? And, what about Ramskill? There's no doubt they're connected, but we don't have any idea about why . . ."

"Agreed . . ."

"I think it's time we figure it out—there has to be a connection between Sanderson, Ramskill, Nathan Moss, and Peyton Maxwell."

"Don't forget Ramskill's wife—she's in the mix now."

Again, Colbie closed her eyes, thinking of connecting threads that may lead them in the right direction. "That's five—and, I'm sticking to my theory there's someone else," she commented as her intuition again took hold. "Someone who's more than capable of keeping plans to himself . . ."

"A man?"

She nodded. "Yes—and, whoever he is, he's ruthless." Her eyelids flickered as if she were watching a movie. "We need to expand . . ."

"Meaning?"

"We need to investigate collectors . . ."

After her latest conversation with Detective Dellinger, Colbie wasted little time infiltrating the archaeological art scene and, although she wasn't a complete dope about ancient relics, she planned to use what ignorance she had to her advantage.

"It's lovely, isn't it?" A middle-aged woman stood next to her, admiring a piece from an age of which Colbie knew little.

"It is—but, I confess, my knowledge of such pieces is only beginning!"

"Oh? You're new to relic art?"

Colbie nodded. "Yes—it's absolutely fascinating!"

The woman agreed, apparently feeling the need to educate. "It's Mayan—such an interesting culture."

Talk about a stroke of luck.

"Really?" Colbie stared at the tiny relic, playing her part. "I heard the Mayan had something to do with blue paint . . ." A pause. "Or, maybe I read it . . ."

"Oh, yes—that's true. They painted those chosen for sacrifice—or, warriors."

"I know—but, why?"

"Strictly for ceremonial purposes, I believe—but, if you want to talk to someone who knows everything about the Mayans, it's Clifford Rasmussen . . ." She turned, then pointed discreetly. "He's right over there . . ."

"I've heard of him!"

"Would you like me to introduce you?"

"Really? I don't know—I don't want to come across like an idiot to someone like him!" As Colbie uttered the words, her stomach turned. "I don't know enough . . ."

"Well, luckily, Clifford Rasmussen loves to hear himself talk—I'm sure he'll tell you everything you want to know. And, then some . . ." She grinned, then gently led Colbie by the arm. "How about if I introduce you, and you can take it from there?"

"Okay . . ."

"You'll be fine! Ask him one question, and he'll be off and running . . ."

Minutes later, Colbie stood with one of the foremost academicians in the archaeology world, hoping to snag useful information. "I feel terrible! How rude of me—I didn't get your colleague's name."

Rasmussen smiled. "That's Bernie—she's the curator of a museum up north."

"Oh!"

"She's here for the conference on Wednesday . . ."

Colbie shifted her position slightly, keeping her eye on the woman who opened the door to opportunity. "She's very nice—she said, however, you're the one to talk to about the Mayan culture. I'm just beginning to study it . . ."

"Formally?"

"Good heavens, no! I do find it interesting however, so I thought I'd come to one of your events . . ."

"Well, you have good timing—the best of the best will be here for the conference. This evening is simply a get-together to relax . . ."

"Can anyone attend?"

Rasmussen eyed her carefully, a twinge of warning making itself known. "Of course—there's a fee, however." His was a comment designed to dissuade—instead, it achieved the opposite.

"Not a problem," Colbie confirmed, aware Rasmussen was holding her at bay. "So, one thing I've been hearing about is the blue paint associated with the Mayan culture . . ."

"It is, indeed, interesting—used only for ceremonial purposes, however. I know there are some of my ilk who believe the Maya somehow had a presence in our state, but I think it's hogwash . . ."

"I read about that—I also read about Richard Sanderson. He was one of the believers, wasn't he?"

"He was . . ." Rasmussen glanced at Bernie as if silently asking her to intervene in a conversation making him uncomfortable.

"Didn't he discover a small statue?"

"He did . . ."

"I'm sure you know—is it on display somewhere? I'd love to see it!"

At that moment, Clifford Rasmussen caught his wife's eye. "I apologize—I'm afraid I must go. It was a pleasure meeting you . . ." With that he met her in a far corner of the room, both leaving shortly after.

"It seems you were having a delightful conversation," Bernie commented, noticing Colbie stood alone.

"We did—but, it was too short! Unfortunately, he had to leave . . ."

"Well, he is a busy man . . ."

Minutes later, Colbie walked out the door, hoping to get a glimpse of Rasmussen and his wife.

No such luck.

Nathan Moss grabbed a beer and a bag of chips, then headed for the couch, propping his feet on the coffee table. Throughout his return trip, he could think of nothing else other than Tabashi Abnal's refusal to acquiesce, and it was clear something had to be done. As difficult as it was to believe, there existed the possibility he needed to change his approach . . .

A tact he found abhorrent.

The sad fact was his trip to the Yucatan was an absolute bust—money down the drain. Yet, if he were to look at things in a positive light, the only good thing he could come up with was his dinner before boarding the plane was palatable.

As he drank and munched, the possibility arose his trip to see Tabashi Abnal wasn't the smartest move—especially since Abnal didn't bite. As disgusted and angry as he was when Nathan left, it wouldn't surprise Moss one bit if his trip came back to bite him in the ass.

Still, he had to consider the facts—if anyone got wind of the info in his journals? Well, let's just say Abnal would be finding a new line of work in a place he wouldn't like. As far as Moss saw it, the archaeologist was pivotal to his plan—without him, Nathan may as well kiss it goodbye.

"What do you know about Clifford Rasmussen?" Colbie took a sip of water, then focused on her laptop screen.

Damion thought for a moment, trying to place the name. "Never heard of him . . ."

"Neither had I until I had a chance to meet him last night . . ."

"Where?"

"At a relic art event—if you recall, we decided to focus on the periphery rather than the obvious."

"I remember—I take it Rasmussen is a collector?"

"Yep—big name. Big bucks . . ."

"How do you know?" If Damion knew anything about Colbie it was her penchant for research—if something got past her scrutiny, she'd kick herself about it until the end of a case.

"I checked him out online after I got home. Not only that, he was dressed in a top-of-the-line, designer suit—it had to have cost thousands."

The detective grinned. "I didn't know you're so well versed in designers . . ."

Colbie laughed, thinking of her last case taking her across the globe into the bowels of the fashion industry. "Don't ask—just believe me when I say the guy likes to look good!"

Damion grinned, his gut telling him it was something he'd enjoy hearing. "Sounds intriguing—a story, perhaps, for a different time." He paused. "So—thoughts?"

"About Rasmussen?" She, too, took a second to think. "I'm not sure he has anything to do with Sanderson's and Ramskill's murders—but, I do feel he's involved with the statue, somehow."

"Did you ask him about it?"

She shook her head. "No—in fact, I didn't really feel that until he walked away from me."

"I suppose it does make sense, however—if Sanderson had something a collector wanted?"

"What would that person do to get it . . ."

"Exactly." Damion scribbled a few notes, the focused again on his screen. "I'll put him through the system . . ."

Minutes later they clicked off, both promising to be available the following day for a quick update session. Neither knew where their new direction would take them, but it was a trail they needed to follow.

Besides, what else did they have?

CHAPTER 17

Tabashi Abnal sat at his small table, laptop ready for his upcoming conversation. It was a decision he had no trouble making for he knew the day would eventually arrive—why he sold his soul, he had no idea. The only thing he knew was he had to make it right. "Detective Dellinger—it's good to see you even if it's not in person!"

"Same to you—I admit, however, I was surprised when I got your message." He paused. "I assume you're okay . . ."

"I will be once we have our conversation—and, please accept my apologies for being so direct. But, it is urgent . . ."

"Not a problem. So, tell me—what's going on?"

For the next thirty minutes, Abnal recounted his visit with Nathan Moss, as well as his attempt to either blackmail, or extort money from him. "I was so pissed, I didn't bother to find out which . . ."

Then, he told him about the journals.

"All of it was there—especially my involvement in covering up Richard Sanderson's murder."

Damion wasn't sure he heard correctly as he watched the man on his screen carefully. "Your involvement?"

Tabashi's shoulders sagged as he fully realized the magnitude of his error in judgment. "Yes, Detective—I couldn't prevent it, but I played a part in how finding Richard's body played out."

"Explain . . ."

"As you know from reports, I was the one called to the scene when one of my workers located Richard's remains . . ."

"I recall."

"Well, that's not exactly true—I already knew he was dead, and had been for about forty-eight hours."

In that moment, Detective Dellinger knew he was going to hear something that would not only answer questions, but lead them to Sanderson's murderer, as well. Ramskill? *If Abnal doesn't mention his name,* he thought as he watched the man on his screen struggle to find words, *there's still a lot of work to do . . .* "I think you should start at the beginning, Mr. Abnal—and, I'll be recording." Damion knew it was a risk, but he needed every bit of evidence he could get."

"I have no objection . . ."

A few seconds later, Damion gave the go-ahead. "Tell me everything . . ."

Spring taking hold, Clifford Rasmussen stood at his kitchen window watching the gardener wrestle with placing new trees in a spot where they'd eventually provide the sense of secrecy he always desired. To be in the public eye as a renowned art collector was always a trial, a little-known fact to those in his circle. A man preferring to keep to himself, he only stepped out when it was expected of him. "There was something about her . . ."

"Did you get her name?"

"No—and, neither did Bernie. I checked . . ."

"What did she look like?"

"Petite—red hair. Short . . ."

Clifford's wife paused just before she took a sip of coffee. "Doesn't sound familiar—what's the big deal?"

He turned, looking at his wife. It was no surprise she wasn't following his train of thought—why he thought their marriage could work was beyond him. Even so, his admirable bent toward traditional values precluded his doing anything about it. She was an albatross, to be sure—a fact that could prove unacceptable sometime in the future. "No big deal— it's simply in my line of work, so it's easy to spot someone who appears completely out of place—you know, a fish out of water."

"Well, perhaps you'll run into her again—if you do, you should ask questions. If she has nothing to hide, she'll be forthcoming—if not, you'll have your answer."

Rasmussen stared at her, quietly wondering if such insight were an anomaly. "You're right—I'll probably never see her again."

His wife stood, then placed her coffee mug in the dishwasher. "See? Now you can go on with your day—problem solved!" With that, she gave him a peck on the cheek, leaving him to his own thoughts . . .

Thoughts coupled with escalating unease.

Tabashi Abnal shifted in his seat, uncomfortable with what he was about to say—yet, he had no choice. "When Richard Sanderson discovered the Mayan statue years back, there were those who thought he was out of his mind . . ."

"You mean trying to link the statue to the Maya's making it to the States?"

Abnal nodded. "Yes—those questioning that particular mindset were astounded he had the audacity to make such a public announcement."

"Why?"

"Because, if true, it changes the narrative, doesn't it?"

Damion thought for a moment. "Indeed, it does . . ."

"And, while it might not matter to the majority of people, it mattered a great deal to those who consider themselves authorities on the culture. In fact, there were several who publicly disregarded his claim as sheer lunacy, refusing to allow such a notion to gain ground . . ."

"Okay—what does that have to do with Sanderson's murder?"

"Think about it, Detective—don't you agree there was much to lose if Sanderson's findings turned out to be true? As an authority in the field, I can tell you it wouldn't be received well—and, there are those who would take action to make certain such an announcement is nothing but false."

"I get your point, Mr. Abnal—but, my question is who? Who would murder Richard Sanderson in order to keep his discovery out of mainstream minds? I assume that's your assertion . . ."

"Yes—and, I knew about the plan long before it happened." He waited, looking for some sort of indication the detective understood the power of his words.

"How long?"

"Months—six, perhaps. I don't recall the exact date I was approached . . ."

"Approached? By whom . . ."

Abnal paused, sweat beginning to form on his forehead. "David Ramskill . . ."

"I'm not sure I understand . . ."

Abnal smiled. "I don't blame you, Detective—it is, indeed, confusing." He paused, smile fading. "It was David

Ramskill who approached me about making sure Richard Sanderson couldn't 'open his yap,' I believe he said."

"About?"

"The statue, of course." Another pause. "You see, Detective, David Ramskill was one of the believers—one of few who strongly suspected what Sanderson touted was true."

"That the Mayans were in Georgia . . ."

"Correct—and, although I don't know for certain, it seemed Ramskill was working with someone else to bring Sanderson down."

"Bringing someone down is a whole lot different than murder, Mr. Abnal . . ."

"Of course, it is, Detective—I'm not denying such a thing."

Damion was quiet, thinking. "Do you have any idea of who the other person was?"

"No—but, it didn't take me long to form the impression it was someone important."

"In what way?"

"You know—a voice within our community. Someone who matters . . ."

"Do you know who killed Richard Sanderson, Mr. Abnal? At that juncture, Damion needed him to get to the point.

"With certainty, no . . ."

"Without certainty?"

"Yes—David Ramskill."

"Why?"

Abnal smiled slightly. "Why do I think so?" He didn't wait for an answer. "Because he had the most to gain. There was no question throughout our community, Detective Dellinger, that David Ramskill was considered a hack by most—a wannabe. His excellence was extremely low, yet, somehow, he managed to make some sort of name for himself. But, only by riding on coattails . . ."

When Damion thought about it, there was some sense to Abnal's story. Ramskill did present himself as someone important, yet—although no one said it outright—it seemed he placed himself with the right people at the right time. "Who's?"

"Coattails? Richard's—oh, Ramskill made it a point to make certain people knew how close he was with Richard, but to those of us who knew Sanderson well? None of it made sense—especially after Richard discovered the statue." Tabashi thought for a moment. "After the announcement of the statue's connection with the blue paint, that's when, I believe, Ramskill recognized his opportunity."

"To do what?"

"Well, with Richard out of the way, Ramskill could carry on his belief of the Maya's presence in the States. Certainly, you can see the value of making a name for one's self by proving such a thing . . ."

As Damion listened, there was no doubt Abnal was being honest—but, what didn't make sense was his being complicit. "You said you knew Richard was murdered two days before his body was found . . . how?"

"David Ramskill surprised me at the dig, requesting a private conversation. Although he was a person I didn't particularly like, I felt it my duty to comply—and, it was then, in privacy, he offered me a great deal to aid him in his plan."

"A plan to do what?"

"At that time, I didn't know—now, there is no doubt my actions set up Richard Sanderson's murder."

"By offering you a great deal, I assume you mean money?"

Abnal nodded. "Yes—he paid me handsomely to make certain Richard was in a certain place at a certain time two days before his body was discovered."

"So—just to make certain I understand you correctly—David Ramskill paid you cash to have Richard Sanderson in a particular place and time forty-eight hours prior to his body being discovered."

"That's correct."

"Did you know Ramskill planned to kill him?"

Tabashi shook his head. "No—in fact, it didn't enter my mind. Now, however . . ."

"Do you believe David Ramskill murdered Richard Sanderson?" As Detective Dellinger figured, it never hurt to confirm previous statements.

"Yes."

"Do you know that for a fact?"

Again, Abnal shook his head. "No—but, it's the only thing that makes sense. That's why I had to contact you . . ."

Damion said nothing, taking notes, even though he would have the recording. Finally, he focused again on the archaeologist. "Okay—let's talk for a moment about Nathan Moss. You said he visited you recently for the purpose of blackmail . . ."

"Yes. He knew all about my involvement in Richard Sanderson's murder. I didn't know it at the time, but he was tracking my every move . . ." He paused. "Ramskill put him up to it, I think—it was no secret he was pulling the strings when it came to Moss's being at the dig in the first place."

"So, as I understand it, Moss compiled three journals, each filled with where you went, what you did, and with whom . . ."

Abnal nodded. "Let's just say my private life is quite different than that of a staid archaeologist . . ."

"You realize I'll get my hands on those journals . . ."

"Yes, Detective—I'm very clear about the consequences of today's conversation."

As Damion watched Abnal slowly crumble into a broken man, he had no doubt Abnal's career would be over. Even if he didn't have first-hand knowledge of Richard Sanderson's murder, his actions most likely led to it. The only question?

What price would he pay?

CHAPTER 18

*C*olbie watched as stragglers took their seats, those eager for speakers to begin their presentations more than slightly irritated by late arrivals. But, what interested her most?

Nathan Moss at the furthest table in the darkest corner of the room.

Thank God I'm on the opposite side, she thought, keeping her eyes on him. As he sat, she couldn't help noticing he spoke to no one, and no one attempted to speak to him. Seemingly invisible to those around him, nothing changed as academicians took turns at the podium—he didn't clap when they were done, offering the same disrespect when they first stood in front of those with a thirst to learn.

During the lunch break, Colbie kept to herself, shrinking into the woodwork as much as she could while never letting Moss out of her sight—and, it wasn't until he made it a point to speak privately to Clifford Rasmussen did the light switch on. The degree of familiarity between the two was intriguing, causing Colbie to question why Rasmussen would waste his time on someone so inconsequential.

Then, as she watched, she realized—they weren't two friends in easy conversation. Clearly, there was more . . .

Something Colbie vowed to understand.

Natasha Ramskill crushed her cigarette into a ceramic ashtray artfully placed on the patio so those against the filthy habit wouldn't notice. Smoking was something her husband barely tolerated, but, since he wasn't around anymore, she embraced her addiction with a happy heart. In fact, the only thing standing in her way of complete freedom was the niggling thought Detective Damion Dellinger might again knock at her door. *If so*, she thought, *I have nothing to hide . . .*

But, when he did stand at her front door once again?

It was best to keep her trap shut.

"Detective—this is a surprise!"

"I'm sure it is—I'd like to speak with you, if you don't mind . . ."

"Well . . ."

Damion's eyes locked with hers. "Let's put it this way—I need to speak with you even if you do mind."

With that, she opened the door. "I hope this will be brief, Detective—I have an appointment."

As Dellinger entered, he couldn't help noticing a change in the decor. "New furniture? It looks nice . . . He glanced at her, noticing the slight smile.

"Thank you—it's always a good feeling to spruce things up a little." She pointed to the living room. "Please—make yourself comfortable."

Thanking her, Damion sat, watching as she sat across from him. "I appreciate your time—that said, I'll be brief." He paused. "Are you familiar with Tabashi Abnal?"

"The archaeologist? Yes—but, only by name. Why?"

It didn't take a genius to figure out Detective Dellinger had no interest in answering her question. "Have you met him," he asked.

"No—I was never interested in socializing with David's colleagues."

"Why not?"

"Because they're not my type, Detective." She paused. "Look at me—am I one to be rooting around in the dirt for something left eons ago?"

"That's not for me to say, Mrs. Ramskill . . ."

"Well, I'll tell you—I'm not. So, whatever friends David had, they weren't friends of mine." She rose. "So, Detective, if that's all . . ."

Damion remained seated, taking notes, then returned his attention to her. "I'm afraid that's not all . . ."

Natasha again sat, clasping her hands in her lap.

"Tell me about your husband's relationship with Richard Sanderson . . ."

"Relationship?"

"Yes, Mrs. Ramskill—relationship. It's no secret they worked together on projects of supreme importance . . ."

"Supreme importance?" Natasha Ramskill chuckled. "You make it sound so . . . imperative."

"To your husband and Sanderson, I can only imagine it was—it was certainly important enough to earn your husband a permanent six feet under." As soon as the words left his mouth, regret pricked his conscience. "I'm sorry . . ." Detective Dellinger paused. "But, don't you want to find out who murdered your husband, Mrs. Ramskill?"

"Well, of course . . ."

"Then, please—tell me what you know. Help me bring your husband's killer to justice . . ."

Natasha extracted a cigarette from an expensive gold case, lighting it before acknowledging Dellinger's question. "What is it you'd like to know, Detective?" *Of course,* she thought as he eyed her, *I have no intention of telling you about the key. Or, the piece of paper I recently retrieved from his pants pocket . . .*

It was the look on her face signaling Damion he was seated across from a woman who mistakenly thought she was in control—the issue then became how long would he allow her to think such a thing. "Let's start with David and the statue with blue paint on it . . ."

Natasha said nothing for a moment—it was a question she didn't anticipate. Prepared to deflect suspicion away from her should the necessity arise, she mistakenly assumed authorities would focus mainly on David's working with Richard Sanderson—not the statue. "The statue? Good heaven's, Detective—what would I possibly care about a statue?"

"Why don't you tell me . . ." Detective Dellinger sat back in his chair, keeping his pen and pad on his lap. "But, what do you say we cut to the chase, Mrs. Ramskill?" He paused, watching her expression carefully. "Did your husband murder Richard Sanderson for the statue?"

Natasha blanched, the cigarette in her hand twitching slightly—even so, she didn't waver. "Surely, you must be joking—David wouldn't harm a fly."

"I'm not talking about flies, Mrs. Ramskill—so, I'll repeat the question, just so you're clear." Again, he paused, gauging her reactions. "Did your husband murder Richard Sanderson?"

Instantly, Natasha Ramskill's eyes darkened with an irritated flash, her face advising of new intent and resolve. She stood, flicking ashes into a glass ashtray, then focused on Dellinger. "I'm afraid it's time for you to go, Detective . . ."

Damion didn't move. "Perhaps," he commented, "I should be as up front as possible. If you don't answer my questions here—in the comfort and privacy of your own home—I'll be more than happy to treat you as my guest at the precinct." A pause. "I'm good either way . . ."

"Well, I'm afraid you'll just have to go through the red tape, Detective."

Damion stood. "You're certain? Because unless you have something to hide, Mrs. Ramskill, what's the harm in telling me what you know?"

"I have nothing to hide!"

"Then, that leaves you in the perfect position to bring someone to justice for your husband's murder—and, Richard Sanderson's." He hesitated, hoping for a flicker of conscience. "Don't you want to find out?"

Her voice a barely audible whisper, Natasha again sat. "Of course . . ."

Dellinger wasn't sure, but he thought a tear formed at the corner of her right eye—if so, she sure as hell wasn't opening the floodgates of grief. "Thank you . . ." He, sat, opened his spiral tablet, then clicked his pen. "You're making the right decision . . ."

She said nothing as she extinguished her cigarette, immediately reaching for another. Of course, the detective noticed, wondering why she was suddenly so nervous—guilt being the obvious first thought.

Then, as if a switch flipped, she leaned forward, cigarette poised elegantly, mimicking a neophyte actress in a forties grade B movie. "What do you want to know?"

So, for the next couple of hours, Damion Dellinger wrote down every word coming out of Natasha Ramskill's mouth.

Too bad every word was a lie.

"You go first . . ." Colbie reached for her cup of tea, dipped the bag a few times, then sat back in her chair focusing on her laptop screen.

"I always go first . . ."

"Okay—I'll go," she laughed, then took a sip, pausing for a moment, recalling her time at the archaeology conference. "It's been a long time since I was around so many academic minds in one room . . ."

"Stuffy?"

"Yes—well, not really. It was more like they were so immersed in their work, personality took a back seat—but, I did manage to walk away with something, I think."

"And, that is . . ."

"Nathan Moss."

"He was there?"

"Oh, yes—and, either the other archaeologists didn't know who he was, or they kept their distance. One or the other . . ."

"Well, he's in the archaeology field, so I imagine many would know who he is . . ."

"Probably—if that's the case, no one paid attention to him. He didn't interact with one person—and, no one tried to talk to him."

"Popular guy . . ."

"No kidding—even more interesting was he didn't make an attempt to speak to anyone. He didn't clap for guest speakers, or anyone else—it almost seemed as if he were trolling."

"For what?"

"I don't know—but, the whole event was weird. A darkness settled on it I can't explain . . ."

"What about Rasmussen?"

"He was there, but he didn't speak to me—in fact, I think he was ignoring me on purpose."

"Maybe he has something to hide . . ."

"That's my thought—so, where does that leave us? We still have Maxwell, Natasha Ramskill, Nathan Moss . . . who else?" Colbie paused, mentally ticking off who was shaking out to being on the top of their suspect list.

"Well, Rasmussen . . ."

"Agreed—so, what about you? How did your conversation with Tabashi Abnal go?"

For the next forty-five minutes, Damion filled Colbie in on the bombshell confession, prompting her to wonder why it took Abnal so long to spill his guts. "He knew from the first time you spoke," she commented. "Why did he purposely keep it from you?"

"I'm not sure, but my guess is he figured silence was the best way to save his own ass. The important thing is he did the right thing . . ."

"What are you going to do?"

"About Abnal? Well—I'm not sure. He said when he set up Sanderson to be at a specific location, he had no idea Ramskill was going to murder him . . ."

"Or, have him murdered—we still don't know if Ramskill did the deed himself. All we have is Abnal's word . . ."

"True—but, as far as Abnal is concerned? I'll have to think about it. My gut tells me it would be a flimsy case, at best, to convict—and, from the look of him, he regrets every second of his involvement."

Colbie was quiet for a moment, thinking. "It would probably be best to have him as a material witness . . ."

"My thought, exactly. But, for now, I want to keep my eye on Natasha Ramskill—she's not about to cough up information that may incriminate her."

"I thought you said she's . . ."

"A cold, calculating shopper? Yes—but, that doesn't make her stupid. Unless I missed something, the lovely Natasha Ramskill is brighter than we give her credit for . . ."

"Well, how about if I surveil?"

Damion paused, thinking of how Colbie's offer would save his department time, and money. "Are you sure you have the time?"

"I'll make time—honestly, though? I'm beginning to feel there's a common thread in this case, and Maxwell, Ramskill, Moss, and Rasmussen are in it big time . . ."

"Same here—someone with a brain is calling the shots."

Again, Colbie was quiet. "I think," she finally commented, "it's time to up our game . . ."

CHAPTER 19

Nathan Moss dimmed the lights, then sat on his couch, three journals carefully placed in front of him, candlelight illuminating the pages just enough to read. Up until Tabashi Abnal squirreled his plan by playing hardball, everything was going as it should—now, he wasn't so sure. There was little question the information contained in his journals was enough to bring down those who considered themselves impervious—but, would they take him seriously?

Apparently not, if Abnal were an accurate indication.

Then again, he couldn't spend time thinking about such things.

Gently, he opened the first journal, reading first words written nearly two years prior. With renewed inspiration, he knew he should be proud of his accomplishments—yet, bolstered pride wasn't what he was seeking.

With misplaced reverence he turned each page, delighted by his ability to pen an accurate chronology of acts he considered abhorrent. The fact Peyton Maxwell was stepping out with David Ramskill was disgusting enough— but, Rasmussen, too? *Won't the archaeology world love that tidbit of information*, he thought as he traced the final words of the first journal with his index finger.

It was certainly a thought worth thinking—with what he knew? Well, it was enough to topple those he considered reprehensible, results reaching far beyond the fringe. It was also a thought serving as unbridled inspiration to do something for which he would always be remembered, sparking him to make a much-needed decision.

Carefully, he gathered his journals, placing them in a fabric tote his grandmother made for him when he was in the sixth grade—it was all he had left of the only person who loved him without judgment. Without assumption.

Without expectation.

Blowing out the candles, tote in hand, he grabbed his coat then headed out the front door. As the saying goes, time was certainly of the essence and, if he were to see his plan to fruition, he sure as hell couldn't be sitting around doing nothing.

An emboldened Nathan Moss had work to do.

Colbie watched as Peyton Maxwell parallel parked at the end of the block, then walked to a small tavern tucked between a laundromat and a rib joint boasting the best baby backs in town. Tailing her from the time she left her apartment, when Maxwell turned toward what many considered the part of town where few wanted to go, Colbie's radar switched to high gear. But, when Maxwell entered a sleazeball bar?

Something was up.

Colbie scanned the area for a spot more conducive to surveillance, but there was none offering proper anonymity. The situation clearly called for patience and, unfortunately, it wasn't one of her strong suits. Luckily, however, she didn't have to wait—within fifteen, Peyton Maxwell pushed through the bar's door with an obvious escalating fury.

Colbie watched as she hurried down the street, clicked the key fob to her car, then climbed in, pounding her fists on the steering wheel the second she closed the door. Whether she were crying, Colbie couldn't tell—but, what she saw clearly through the binos was a subsequent look of steely determination. About to follow, Colbie glanced at the bar at the precise moment Natasha Ramskill walked through the front door, scanned the area as if someone may be looking, then disappeared around the corner.

What the hell are they doing here? Glancing at Peyton's car, Colbie pulled from the curb, turning at the corner where Natasha vanished. Slowing as a silver sedan pulled onto the street from the bar's back-alley parking lot, Colbie watched as Natasha gunned it as if fueled by a fear rocking her soul.

Intuition kicking into high gear, Colbie tailed her from a distance, a recent conversation with Dellinger cycling through her mind. They figured Maxwell and Natasha were acquaintances simply because of the small, academic circles they enjoyed—how well they knew each other, however, was conjecture. *Clearly,* Colbie thought as she kept the silver sedan in sight, *there's something they don't want anyone to know . . .*

Nathan Moss reached his destination just as twilight turned—having been there many times previous, he knew exactly where to park without risk of discovery. If there were lights on? His target was home. If not?

It could be a long wait.

As he saw it, such a mission required patience and a temperate soul—both virtues he possessed, yet were traits which most chose not to see. It was always something sticking in his craw, too—if only people would give him a chance, he could prove how important he could be to their existence. Perhaps it was a lofty ideal never to achieve, but that knowledge certainly didn't prevent him from trying. All he had to do was prove his allegiance to those who mattered, and his life would be complete—considering, of course, they were amenable.

Five minutes or so after getting comfortable, a light switched on in what Moss knew was the living room. Granted, it had been a while, but, if he knew his target as well as he thought, heavy drapes on the picture window would remain open, revealing sporadic city lights as they flicked on.

Then, it was time.

Quietly, he approached the door, three leather journals tucked in the crook of his arm, much the same as when he visited the lovely Peyton Maxwell and Tabashi Abnal. Again, they provided comfort, the soft leather a luxurious feel he particularly enjoyed.

As he stood at the front door, energy coursed through him, erasing any doubt—his moment was meant to be, setting in motion a series of events capable of destroying lives. At least, that's what he hoped—the way things were going?

A crapshoot.

With a long, deep breath, he knocked, a hollow sound resonating through the foyer as he remembered. Moments later, footsteps—then, the charming, familiar creak as the door slowly opened. "Moss! What the hell are you doing here?"

"Surprised to see me?"

"Of course, I'm surprised! I didn't think you were that stupid . . ." Clifford Rasmussen glared at him, rising anger increasing its grip. "What do you want?"

"I know it might not be the most opportune time, but I need just a few minutes . . ."

"For what?"

Moss clutched the journals tighter, their comfort igniting the moment. "I have something you may be interested in . . ."

Rasmussen eyed the journals. "What the hell are those?"

Nathan smiled. "Your life . . ."

"What? What are you talking about?"

With that, Rasmussen stepped back to close the door, Moss meeting the challenge by placing his foot between the door and the jamb. "You're making a hasty decision, Clifford—perhaps you should rethink your position."

There was something in Nathan Moss's tone— accompanied by the cold, vacant look in his eyes—cueing Clifford Rasmussen to open the door. If Moss had something to show him, it was in Rasmussen's best interest to know what it was—fewer surprises that way. "Make it quick—I have things to do."

A slight smile tugging on his lips, Moss accepted the invitation to step inside, delighting in the fact Clifford Rasmussen's life was about the change. "Thank you. This won't take long . . .

"I tailed her to her house—after she opened the garage then closed the door, I didn't see her again. Nothing through the windows, either . . ."

"Maybe I should have a chat with the bartender . . ."

"Good idea—Maxwell wasn't there very long, but it will be interesting to find out how many times they've been there." Again, Colbie envisioned Peyton's face as she headed for her car. "She sure was pissed about something . . ."

"What about Ramskill?"

"The same, judging from the way she sped out of the parking lot and, from the way she was driving? My guess is she wasn't happy . . ."

Damion hesitated, thinking of his next move. "I'll head to the bar . . ."

"Have you been there before?"

"No—but, I doubt it's different than any other sleazebag outfit." Another pause. "I'll get in touch in the morning . . ."

Colbie agreed and they clicked off, both mentally outlining what each had to accomplish. Clifford Rasmussen still remained a mystery outside of his collector reputation, little written about his personal life. *Perhaps*, she thought, closing her laptop, *it's time I pay Mr. Rasmussen an official visit . . .*

"Don't make yourself comfortable . . ." Clifford glared at his unexpected guest as Moss tried to figure out where to sit. "You have five minutes . . ."

"Well, I suspect I'll need a little more time, but we can certainly play it by ear . . ."

Rasmussen watched as Moss arranged the journals carefully on the coffee table in front of the vintage couch. "What the hell are you doing?"

Nathan smiled, then graciously gestured for Clifford to sit. "Please—start with the journal on your left. You'll clearly understand it's the best starting point as you continue to read . . ."

Rasmussen glanced at Moss, then again at the journals. "I don't know what the hell you're up to, Moss . . ."

"You'll soon understand." Again, he gestured to the couch. "Please—sit."

Clifford hesitated then obeyed, completely aware of the irony. Nathan Moss telling him what to do in his own home?

No one would've believed it.

Impatiently, he snatched the first journal from the table, disrespecting its importance—an act Moss regarded a personal affront. Quickly scanning the first few pages, as its contents became clear, he glanced at Moss, then back at the pages. Then, for the next thirty minutes he read, not looking up, his face turning ashen then flushed as he fully realized its consequences.

Of course, Nathan was thrilled Rasmussen actually took the time to read past the first few pages—a courtesy Peyton Maxwell and Tabashi Abnal refused to extend. Had they done so, they would've learned of certain options Moss chose to offer—choices keeping them out of the limelight, as well as the authorities' crosshairs.

"You're playing with fire, Moss . . ." Clifford threw the third journal on the table, allowing Nathan the opportunity to retrieve them.

"Fire?" Nathan paused, enjoying the moment. "I don't think so . . ." Another brief pause accompanied by an insincere smile. "You see, Clifford, in addition to the information in these journals . . ." He clutched them tighter as if instinctively knowing they were in danger. "It's only a fraction of what I know . . ."

"What are you talking about?"

"It's simple, really—in my quest to become a published author within the archaeological community, I realized one thing . . ."

"And, what was that?"

"Those at the top must relinquish their positions . . ."

Rasmussen continued to glare at him, all the while thinking Nathan Moss was a flippin' nut. "For what reason, Moss? So you can take their place?"

"Well, that—as well as the satisfaction knowing I'm in control."

"Control? You?" For the first time since Nathan Moss arrived, Clifford smiled. Then, he stood. "Get out! And, if you come near me again, I'll contact the authorities!"

Although Moss doubted that was the case, Rasmussen's reaction was exactly as expected. He, too, stood, then headed for the front door, journals held close to his body. Suddenly, he turned, eyeing the man he despised. "I'm surprised you're being so foolish, Clifford—not hearing me out, I mean . . ." A pause. "Foolish, indeed . . ."

CHAPTER 20

*P*eyton Maxwell reached for a tissue. "It's only a matter of time . . ." She paused, regret filling her soul. "It wasn't supposed to be like this . . ."

"Oh, for God's sake! Stop sniveling!" Natasha listened as Peyton blew her nose, then took a long drink of water. "They don't know shit . . ."

"Really? Then how come that investigator showed up at my place? Not once—twice!" She paused, stripping another tissue from the box as she suddenly gained a backbone. "I tried telling you, but you wouldn't listen!"

"Listen to what? Your irrational fear?" In that moment, Natasha Ramskill realized she partnered with the wrong person—one who could quickly become an albatross. "Just keep your mouth shut—as long as we stick to the same story, they can't touch us!"

Peyton, however, wasn't so sure. "Well, as of now? I'm off their radar . . ."

"Meaning?"

"I'm out . . ."

Natasha laughed, quite enjoying the young woman's misguided bravado. "Oh, please—it's a little late for that, don't you think?"

Silence.

"Besides, you're already in this up to your pretty little neck—if you do something stupid?" She paused. "Well, let's just say I don't recommend it . . ."

"Are you threatening me?"

Another chuckle. "Please—I wouldn't waste my time. As I said, your best choice is to stick with our plan . . ."

Peyton Maxwell said nothing, beginning to realize if she wanted to get herself out of such a colossal mess, the time had come to keep such plans to herself. Trust was obviously something in short supply and, if Natasha Ramskill were involved, it was a pretty good bet she'd be thinking only of herself.

"Don't call me again," Peyton ordered as she clicked off, wondering about her next move. *This was never part of the plan*, she thought, tossing her cell on the couch. One thing was certain—if she decided to travel the same path, her view of life could change considerably.

One she wouldn't particularly enjoy . . .

Detective Dellinger sat in his car, reviewing his notes. According to Colbie, she witnessed Peyton Maxwell and Natasha Ramskill at the bar earlier that day—although, not together. Even so, it was enough to warrant serious consideration the two women did, in fact, meet—for what purpose was the question.

Scanning the area as he got out of his car, it made no sense for two, well-educated women to meet at such a dive— unless, of course, they had something to hide. Although Dellinger hadn't the opportunity to meet Peyton in person, if she were anything like Natasha Ramskill . . . well, let's just say it wasn't a good thing. Trust? None. He was more than certain everything coming out of her mouth was a bald-faced lie.

Moments later he pulled on the door, stepping into the bar's dank, dark atmosphere, those submerged in self-pity eyeing him warily as he headed for the bartender. "Detective Damion Dellinger," he commented, flashing his identification, not waiting for a response. "If you have a minute, I'll appreciate it . . ."

The bartender nodded. "Give me a sec . . ." After making certain his patrons were happy, he led the detective to a far corner away from curious ears. "How can I help?"

Dellinger took two photographs from his pocket. "Do you know either of these women?"

"Yep—both of 'em. They were in here today . . ."

"Have they been here before?"

"Nope—first time. At least, I haven't seen 'em . . ."

"You're sure?"

"Look at 'em—do they look like they belong in a dive like this? I'd remember . . ."

Detective Dellinger tried not to smile. "Good point . . . do you know how long they were here?"

The bartender nodded. "Not even fifteen minutes—didn't drink nothin', neither . . ."

"Did you happen to hear what they were saying?"

Another nod. "The blonde said she was sick of the whole damned thing, but I don't know what they were talking about. Then, the dark-haired woman said she . . ."

"The blonde?"

"Yeah—better be getting her priorities straight." He paused, looking again at the photographs. "That was it—the blonde got pissed, and stormed out the door."

"What about the other one?"

"She left . . ."

"Immediately?"

"Pretty much . . ."

After speaking with the bartender for a few more minutes, Detective Dellinger stepped into the humid, Georgia evening convinced Natasha Ramskill had more than a passing interest in living life sans her husband. In his mind?

Top of the list.

The thing about lies?

It's hard to keep up, making little difference who or what stands in their way as they gain momentum, destroying those in their path. And, though Peyton Maxwell may have laced her lies with enough truth to deflect attention, there was little doubt there'd be a reckoning. So, when Colbie Colleen stood at her door for the third time, there seemed no reason to keep up the charade—depending, of course, on why the feisty redhead wanted to talk. "I have nothing more to add to what I told you before," she offered as they sat at her glass dining table.

"Well, I'm sorry, Peyton—but, I think you know much more than you told me." A pause as she watched the young archaeologist's face. "In fact, I know you do . . ."

An uncomfortable silence settled as Peyton decided which fork in the road to travel—one of truth, justice, and the American way?

Or, one of lies, deceit, and a whole lot of money?

It was a choice she didn't relish, though she knew her mind was made up the second she hung up from her call with Natasha. Still, she couldn't quite get the words out of her mouth. "I don't know what you're talking about . . ."

Peyton's voice pitched higher, cueing Colbie to escalating stress. "Of course, you do—so, what can you tell me about your friendship with Natasha Ramskill?"

Peyton reached for a half-finished bottle of water, knowing she should offer Colbie something as well, but didn't. "Natasha? What about her?"

"Well, I know you met with her earlier today at a bar neither one of you would enter if it weren't for dire circumstances . . ."

"You were following me?"

Colbie nodded. "Detective Dellinger was going to speak with the bartender to acknowledge what we now know . . ."

Peyton swiped at a few strands of errant, curly, hair. "And, what is that . . ."

"You and Natasha Ramskill know more about David Ramskill's murder than either of you are letting on . . ." She paused. "So, if you continue down that road, I'm sure you realize I can't help you . . ."

"Help me?"

Again, Colbie nodded, her intuition telling her Peyton Maxwell was close to calling it quits—whatever 'it' was. "I think, Peyton, you got caught up in something way out of your league . . ."

A sniffle.

"And, I also think you don't know how to get out of it . . ."

Another sniffle as Peyton reached for a tissue, saying nothing, listening to every word.

"Honestly—I think you know who murdered Richard Sanderson, and David Ramskill. Is that right?"

Again, Peyton said nothing for a few moments, weighing her options until, finally, she spoke. "I don't know who killed Richard . . ."

"What about David Ramskill?" Colbie leaned back in her seat, watching a young woman begin to crumble. "What do you know?"

But, seconds later, Peyton Maxwell stood, then headed toward the door. "I have nothing else to say . . ."

Convo over.

CHAPTER 21

*A*lthough sordid, it was somewhat fitting Nathan Moss's body was discovered not far from his university haunts—a statement of sorts, don't you think? At least that's what Colbie and Damion thought when they received word, Dellinger calling Colbie as he headed for the scene. "I'm a few minutes out . . ."

"Are you sure it's him?"

"Well, there's a driver's license with his name on it, and its stuck in his teeth . . . so, I'm pretty sure."

"Geez!"

"I know—it says a lot about the person who stuffed him in with the garbage."

"Control . . ."

"That—and, he wants us to know who died at his hands."

"His hands? What's to say it wasn't a woman?"

Damion glanced left and right, turning slowly into traffic. "Nothing—but, it's pretty hard to toss a grown man in a dumpster. Especially a tall one . . ."

Colbie agreed, but something definitely wasn't feeling right. "How far from the university?"

"Fifteen minutes—maybe a little more. It's definitely an area well known to students as well as faculty . . ." A pause. "I'm here . . ."

With a promise to keep her in the loop, they rang off as Damion approached the scene, scanning the area for onlookers or anyone appearing out of place as he joined his junior detective. "Who found him?"

"We don't know—an anonymous call."

Just what Dellinger didn't want to hear—and, peering in the dumpster, there was no mistaking the wiry archaeologist. "Anything around the scene?"

"Nothing—the only thing is the driver's license stuck between his teeth. In fact, I couldn't read it because he's in the bottom of the dumpster—so, I took a picture with my phone." Pulling his cell from his pocket, Detective Mark Baldwin tapped the screen, enlarging the photo. "I got lucky because he's face up—it's him."

Nathan Moss lay on his back, eyes open, his face listing slightly to his right toward a partially opened trash bag. Beside him were three piles of leather, offering little in the way of immediate information. "Secure the scene," Dellinger ordered, not taking his eyes from Moss.

"Done . . ."

For the following hour, Dellinger's men combed the area, nothing leading them where they needed to go—to whomever did the deed. Even so, the detective already suspected a few familiar to him, instinctively knowing it was foolish to think Moss's murder was at the hands of anyone outside of his circle. Not only that, there was a stench about the whole damned thing, leading the detective to believe things were heating up.

Leaving Baldwin in charge and tapping his cell screen on the way to his car, he connected with Colbie. "We're close," he advised as he pulled away from the scene.

"I think you're right . . ." Colbie was quiet for a moment, thinking of her time with Peyton Maxwell. "I talked to Peyton—half-way through our conversation, I thought she was going to come clean. But, no such luck—she kicked me out."

"Not the most brilliant move . . ."

"Agreed, but it does seem to corroborate our thought she's complicit . . ."

Detective Dellinger was quiet, thinking about Moss, and how Maxwell had no practical use for him. "I think it's time to start turning the screws—how do you feel about your putting the pressure on Natasha? I'll do the same with Peyton—both might crack if someone new interviews them."

"Good idea—I was planning on talking to Emma this afternoon, but that can wait."

"Emma? Sanderson's sister?"

"Yes—but, it's not important. I wanted to talk to her about Richard's time before he began working at the university. It dawned on me we haven't really delved into life before 'professor-hood' . . ."

"Makes sense—but, I think we need to turn the heat up on the two ladies who met clandestinely in a rat-trap bar. If it's okay with you, I agree Emma can wait . . . "

Colbie paused, scratching a few notes on her legal pad. "I'll try to get time with Natasha today—if not, I'll let you know."

"Same here—I'm not giving Maxwell the courtesy of advance notice."

Both agreeing to meet at seven that evening for dinner, as Colbie rang off, she couldn't help feeling as if something were about to give. Closing her eyes, she took a few deep breaths, allowing her body and mind to relax, taking her to a place where she truly felt at home. Instantly, images began to form, different from any she experienced previously.

Moments later, however, she suddenly opened her eyes, an icy chill settling on her. A malevolence. Evil. Then, a cold hand touching the top of her head as a priest might bless a young child.

Knowing she was in the presence of something she was meant to understand, Colbie also knew it was there for a reason—and, with it, came a message.

She watched as a light grey mist began to form in the corner of her living room, then scooted up the wall and across the ceiling until directly above her. Not looking up, she sensed its presence as it began to dissipate, finally vanishing into the wall behind her. "I know you're here for a reason," she said softly. "What is it I need to know?"

Again, she closed her eyes, watching images streak in and out of her mind's eye. All she could focus on, however, was one thing . . .

A Mayan statue with traces of blue paint.

Damion sat back in his chair, focusing directly on Colbie. "You feeling okay?" For the first time since they met, she wasn't her usual, chipper self.

"I'm fine—just a little out of sorts."

"Because?" Of course, he knew he shouldn't pry, but he couldn't help himself. "Anything I can do?"

"Good heavens, no!" A pause. "I don't know—things just feel weird, that's all . . ."

"Weird how?"

It was then she told him of her experience earlier that day. "I've been dealing with my intuitive abilities for my entire life, and what happened was a defining moment in our investigation—I'm sure of it."

Damion noticed their server heading toward their booth, shaking his head almost imperceptibly as she approached— it wasn't a good time. "I'm not sure what you mean . . ."

Colbie sipped her wine before continuing. "I know this is going to sound weird, but I'm convinced the apparition I experienced today was Nathan Moss . . ."

"What?"

"I know—but, it felt like him, and there was a darkness about it I didn't like." She paused, recalling their time with Moss early in the investigation. "The first time I met him, I knew there was something much deeper than a young archaeologist trying to make a name for himself . . ."

"Well, that's probably true—making a name for himself, I mean."

"I'm sure it is, but . . ."

Damion waited patiently as Colbie tried to make sense of things. "If you felt something were really off—more than we discussed—why didn't you mention it?"

It was a mistake Colbie didn't particularly want to admit. Still, it was her pattern—saying nothing when she knew better. Nearly a decade prior while in the neophyte stages of her relationship with Brian, it drove him nuts when she wouldn't come clean about things she knew to be true. Finally, however, as years passed, he understood.

Colbie Colleen was seldom sure about herself.

Placing her wine on the table, she sat back with a gentle sigh. "I wish I knew . . ."

A moment for introspection? Perhaps. Few times in one's life, do we have the opportunity to witness self-deprecation with targeted precision and pinpointed accuracy. It was something Damion hated to see, and he had the smarts to know when to clam up. "Are you ready to order," he asked as he topped off her glass.

For a brief second, he thought he caught a glimpse of sadness in her eyes. "The usual?"

Colbie laughed, but without her usual delight. "You know me that well?"

"Not really—but, prime rib is a pretty good guess, don't you think?"

With a smile she agreed, solemnity of the previous moments passing. "So—enough about me. What did you find out about Moss?"

"Nothing much, so far—the scene was clean." The detective paused, thinking about the dumpster. "There were three piles of leather beside him . . ."

"Leather? That's weird . . ."

"It's that really soft leather—you know, the kind writers use."

"You mean a journal?"

Damion grinned. "Exactly!"

"Well, if they were journals . . ."

"I know where you're going—good idea, except there were no pages," Damion commented as the server approached with appetizers.

As soon as she was gone, Colbie popped a crab-stuffed won ton in her mouth. "I'm starving!" Then, another. "Okay— I'm good for now!" Instantly, she changed gears. "No pages? Were they ripped out?"

"It seems so—there were bits of paper in the dumpster, but none had writing on it."

"I assume they're already at the lab . . ."

"Yep—so, all we can do is wait. In the meantime, though, we need to ramp up—first thing in the morning, I'm hauling Peyton Maxwell in for formal interrogation."

"Seriously?"

"Damned straight! It's time—and, from what you told me about your last conversation with her, I don't think it's going to take much to get her to spill her guts."

Colbie nodded. "You're probably right—she's a smart cookie, and I don't think she relishes the thought of spending time in prison with new roommates."

"Let's hope so—because, if she's involved in any way, we're coming in strong. It won't be pretty . . ."

"It shouldn't be . . ."

Just as Damion was about to tackle the topic of Colbie's chat with Natasha Ramskill—which didn't happen—his cell buzzed. "Hold that thought," he grinned as its screen bloomed to life. "What?" He read the text message again. "You're never going to believe this . . ." Then, a third time. "Well, since it's you, maybe you will . . ."

"Alright, already! What am I not going to believe?"

He stood, signaling their dinner was over—at least for him. "Who do you think is at the precinct right now wanting to see me?"

"Three guesses?"

"Just one—I have to go."

She, too, stood, instinctively knowing she would be dining alone if she chose to stay. "Then, enlighten me . . ."

"The lovely Peyton Maxwell . . ."

Within the hour, Detective Dellinger sat across from the young archaeologist, notepad open, Detective Baldwin taking his place standing against the wall, arms crossed. "So, Ms. Maxwell—this is quite a surprise. I'm assuming you have something you wish to discuss . . ."

Well, that was all it took, and saying she dissolved into tears doesn't do it justice. "Your partner said if I didn't cooperate, she wouldn't be able to help me . . ."

"My partner?"

She nodded. "Colbie Colleen . . ."

"When did she tell you that—recently?"

Another nod.

The detective watched her carefully, then glanced at his junior detective. Dellinger was less than aboveboard when it came to working with the psychic redhead, the disapproving look in Baldwin's eyes duly noted. For the first time, the junior detective knew there was someone else in the picture.

"Well, then it certainly appears we have much to discuss." Damion turned his attention to Detective Baldwin. "Please bring Ms. Maxwell a cold water . . ."

There was, of course, typical subterfuge associated with the request—DNA was always a good thing. But, what he really wanted?

A few minutes alone with Peyton Maxwell.

Well, not really alone—the two-way mirror was obvious. But, Damion had a strong sense of Peyton's unwillingness to talk with someone else in the room even though she didn't say.

"Okay—I'm going to make this brief. Do you know who murdered David Ramskill, Ms. Maxwell?" He kept his eyes on her as she struggled with how much she should say.

"Not for sure . . ."

"So, you suspect someone . . ."

Again, Peyton was silent, her eyes cast to the floor. "I think so . . ."

"And, that is?"

Suddenly, she looked up, bravado making its first appearance. "Natasha Ramskill."

If there were ever a choir-from-the-heavens moment, that was it. "What makes you think is was her?"

"What makes me think so? Because when I met her in the bar that day, she threatened me . . ."

"Threatened? In what way?"

Peyton dabbed at her eyes, then swiped her nose. "She said if I said anything about her involvement in David's murder, she'd make sure I paid for it."

Dellinger was quiet, watching, waiting for her to continue. When she didn't, he guided the questioning gently, his gut telling him it was the best approach. "Did you kill David Ramskill?"

Suddenly, her eyes met his, terror obscuring their underlying beauty. "No!"

"Ms. Maxwell—did you have anything to do, at all, with his murder? Anything . . ."

Watching a pierced soul disintegrate is never pleasant, but Dellinger's heart dropped a little when he realized how fragile she truly was. "If you know anything, Peyton, this is the time to tell me . . ."

With that she straightened a little, hoping for a stronger backbone. "She made me do it . . .

"Natasha?"

A nod.

"Do what?"

"Have an . . . well . . ."

"A relationship?"

Another nod.

Damion looked up as Baldwin entered with the bottle of water, his look warning the detective to say nothing. "Excellent!" He took the bottle, then placed it in front of Peyton. "I know this is difficult—please, take your time."

Immediately, she opened it, taking a delicate sip. "Does he have to be in here?"

"I think it's appropriate . . ."

She glanced at the water bottle. "DNA?"

"Do I need it?"

She shook her head. "No. I'll tell you everything . . ."

CHAPTER 22

When delving into a world of deceit and destruction, things tend to get a little unbecoming. Unwieldy. Unfortunate. And, so it was when Peyton Maxwell became a liability rather than an ally. While never pleasant when relationships turn, there comes a time to take certain measures, and Natasha Ramskill was keenly aware time was running out.

Purposely and strategically positioned across from the precinct parking lot, she snapped photos as Peyton walked down the steps looking both directions—as if someone were interested—before heading for her car. Unsure of how she would use such damning photos, of one thing she was certain . . .

She and Ms. Maxwell needed to have a little chat.

Careful not to arouse suspicion, she followed several cars behind once Peyton pulled into traffic, tailing her until she turned off the highway, heading toward tobacco farmland. Finally, she slowed, pulling into a long lane lined with pecan trees.

Trying not to look as she drove past, Natasha couldn't help herself.

What the hell is she doing . . . here?

"Do you believe her?"

Detective Dellinger threw his pen on the desk, then focused his attention on Baldwin. "I do—I think it's the first time she told the truth since this whole damned thing started."

"I don't know . . ." Thick, understandable tension filled Dellinger's office, cueing Damion he needed to be honest with his junior detective. "I suppose you're wondering who Maxwell was talking about . . ."

"It crossed my mind . . ."

"Well—Colbie Colleen. She's a behavioral profiler, who just happens to have the gift . . ."

"The gift?"

"Yeah—you know, psychic."

Baldwin didn't say anything for a moment, allowing his boss's revelation to settle—he suspected something, but that wasn't it. "You're working with a psychic?"

So, for the next twenty minutes, Dellinger filled him in on working with Colbie a few years prior, finally convincing the young detective of her worth. "If it weren't for her? We'd still be working on it . . ." And, that's where he left it—there was no reason to tell him about their serendipitous meeting in the Yucatan.

Or, anything else.

"First on our list?" Damion again focused squarely on his junior detective. "I want to know everything about those piles of leather next to Moss's body . . ." He paused, thinking out loud about Colbie's comment. "If they were journals . . ."

"I'll check Amazon first . . ."

Detective Dellinger nodded. "My guess is Moss wouldn't buy anything too extravagant in the leather department. You should also look for really soft leather—kind of like suede, but not really."

"That clears it up . . ." Baldwin grinned, hoping to lighten things up a little.

"Damned straight, it does!" Damion returned the smile. "Now get your ass out of here . . ."

Fuming as she stepped across the threshold, Natasha slipped her key in the lock, threw her keys on the foyer table, then crossed to the liquor cabinet, pouring herself a stiff scotch. Moments later?

A sharp rap on the front door.

Checking her watch, she realized it was a time when most don't come calling, so, when she peered around the long, slender, vertical window by the massive door, she was surprised to see someone she didn't recognize. "Yes," she asked, opening the door slightly.

"Mrs. Ramskill?"

A prolonged hesitation. "Yes . . ." She stared at the petite redhead, trying to place where she saw her previously. "Who wants to know?"

"My name is Colbie Colleen . . ."

Natasha's stomach sank, instantly knowing the woman standing on her front porch was the investigator Peyton Maxwell mentioned. "What can I do for you?"

Although Colbie stood before her hoping for an invitation to enter, it wasn't to be—Natasha Ramskill's guard was up in full force. "I need to talk to you about your husband's murder . . ."

"If you're a cop, show me your I.D."

"I'm not a cop . . ." It was then Colbie confirmed what she suspected before she got out of her car—Natasha wasn't about to tell anyone anything.

"Then, get the hell off of my porch, or I'll call the cops!"

"Aren't you interested in learning who murdered your husband, Mrs. Ramskill?"

"Of course . . ."

"So am I—so, if you have certain information, maybe we can figure it out."

Natasha eyed Colbie with a prolonged, scrutinizing glare, recognizing her windfall opportunity. "You're right—I'm sorry I was so rude. Please, come in . . ."

Within a couple of minutes, they sat in the Ramskill living room, Colbie understanding exactly what Dellinger meant when he said Natasha loved shopping—exquisite pieces, yet none of it in keeping with the decorating style of an archaeologist. "Thank you. I promise not to take up much of your time . . ."

"What I can tell you, Ms. Colleen, is I already spoke to Detective Dellinger. I don't have anything else to add . . ."

The truth? Of course not. But, it was a dandy lead-in to a conversation she chose to control.

"Maybe not, but it's certainly worth a try." Colbie paused, playing her part. "Can you think of anyone who would want your husband out of the picture?"

"No, of course not!"

"No one?"

Natasha hesitated. "Well . . ."

Colbie tuned in as she watched Natasha's face, knowing the performance she was giving was topnotch—unfortunate for her, however, Colbie's was better. "I know this whole thing is really tough on you—I mean, here David is murdered, and all eyes turn to you. That's why I'm trying to figure things out . . ."

"Me? Is that what Detective Dellinger thinks?"

"Well—there isn't anyone else, really. He has to start somewhere . . ."

Natasha stood, eyes flashing. "Then tell him to dig into Peyton Maxwell! She's the one who did it!"

Colbie, too, stood. "Peyton?"

"Of course, it was her! She and David . . ."

Colbie said nothing, waiting to see if Natasha would say anything else.

She didn't.

"You mean they were having a—relationship?" Better not to call it exactly what it was . . .

"For the last year—and, if she thinks I don't know about it?"

"I understand your anger and disappointment—but, that doesn't make Peyton Maxwell a killer."

With an unladylike snort, Natasha lit a cigarette, then took a deep drag. "It does in my book!"

Colbie waited until she calmed down, then guided Natasha in the direction she needed to go. "Do you know for a fact, Mrs. Ramskill, Peyton killed David?"

A nod.

"How do you know?"

"I just do . . ."

"I'm afraid I need something a little more concrete than that . . ."

"You want concrete?" A pause. "How about this—she asked me to meet her in some Godforsaken bar to tell me about her relationship with David! She threatened to tell the cops I killed David to throw me under the bus for something she did!"

"Colbie nodded. "I suspected as much—not all of that, of course, but Peyton Maxwell's been on my radar for a while now." A little empathy, she figured, always goes a long way.

"She should be . . ."

Suddenly, Colbie headed for the door knowing she needed to talk to Dellinger before delving further. "I think I have everything I need," she commented. "Thank you. I'll let myself out . . ."

Natasha watched her go, her radar in high gear.

Everything you need, my ass . . .

CHAPTER 23

*M*orning dawned and, by the time the sun made itself known when rising above the trees, Peyton sat at the small table, tears spilling. "There's trouble . . ."

A glare. "What kind of trouble . . ."

"They're getting close . . ."

"Who?"

"The cops! Who else?"

Of course, there was no doubt the authorities would come snooping—to expect otherwise? A foolish thought, indeed. "You talked to them?"

Peyton nodded. "I had no choice."

"Bull—you always have a choice." A pause. "So, tell me—which choice did you make?" Although she asked the question, there was no doubting the young woman's answer.

An answer capable of ruining everything.

"I had to tell them—no matter what happens to me, I can't live like this!" Debilitating silence settled as the archaeologist's words sank in. "I'm sorry . . ."

"Get out!"

Peyton jumped to her feet, tears streaming, staining her cheeks. "What did you expect me to do?" With that she hurried to the door, not caring if she slammed the screen door on her way out. It wasn't until she reached her car and was down the road, out of sight, did she check in. "Did you hear?"

A voice crackled. "All of it . . ."

"I couldn't stay any longer!"

Detective Mark Baldwin listened to the anguish in her voice, a part of him disliking what they needed her to do. "You did just fine, Peyton.

You did just fine . . ."

"She was exactly as you said . . ." Colbie paused for a second, recalling her conversation with Natasha Ramskill. "But, you missed one thing . . ."

"What's that?"

"She's a liar . . ."

Damion said nothing, Colbie's observations cementing what he knew to be true.

"There's no doubt about what she was trying to do," she continued, pausing for a second for Damion to jump in. When he didn't, she realized he was listening to every word. "It took her about two seconds to throw Peyton Maxwell under the bus . . ."

"Did she know who you were?"

"No—if she did, she wouldn't have opened the door."

"Did you tell her?"

"My name? Of course—it was fun watching her trying to figure out how to play it!"

The detective chuckled. "Same here . . ."

"Meaning?"

"Well—although my conversation with Maxwell wasn't as entertaining as your's with Natasha, we achieved the same thing."

"What do you mean?"

"She cracked the second I opened my mouth—and, although she was more hesitant to do so than Natasha, by the time she walked out of the precinct door . . ."

"How long was she there?"

"Only a few hours—but, let me finish," he laughed. "You're going to love it!"

"Okay, okay—what happened?"

A teasing pause. "Like I was saying, by the time she left, she was wired for sound."

"What? Seriously?"

"Oh, yes—taking Natasha Ramskill down was the only thing on her mind when she left."

Colbie was quiet, thinking of obvious differences. "Did you believe her?"

Again, Damion chuckled. "Baldwin asked me the same thing—so, I'll tell you what I told him." A pause. "I think it's the first time she's been truthful with us since she landed on our radar . . ."

"Have you heard from her? Since the wire?"

"Baldwin just checked in . . ."

"And?"

"Her conversation was brief, but there's no mistaking culpability on some level . . ."

"Maxwell—and, who else?"

For the first time in their working together on the current case, Damion felt the exhilarating thrill of being on the right track. The scent was strong. Fresh. Recent. "I hope you're sitting down . . ."

"Damion!"

"Emma."

"What? Emma Sanderson?" Colbie said nothing for a moment as she sat back in her chair, completely stunned. "What does she have to do with anything? Other than being Richard's sister, of course . . ."

"I'm not sure—Baldwin's on his way back."

"Let me know . . ."

The fact Peyton was making overtures to authorities didn't bode well, and Natasha damned well knew it—and, it was then she realized she had a decision to make. Do something about it? Or, let it slide until she could think of a way to make circumstances work to her advantage . . .

It was, however, unacceptable to think Peyton Maxwell shouldn't pay for her obvious defection—and, Natasha suspected her colleagues would agree if she chose to inform them. And, that was her conundrum—take care of unfinished business on her own? Or, enlist help . . . either way, there would be a price to pay.

A regrettable truth.

Certainly, she's not smart enough to watch her own back, she thought, pulling a bottle of Jack Daniels from the kitchen cabinet. *If Moss is any indication, our plan is working—what's the harm in adding one more?* Irritated, she tossed ice into a rocks glass, then topped it with Tennessee's finest, swirling the silky, burnished liquid with the frosty cubes.

Nothing. Nothing, at all . . .

"She wasn't there long . . ." Baldwin commented as he cued up the surveillance file. "But—as you'll hear—it was long enough . . ." Tapping the keyboard, he stepped back, not wanting to distract Dellinger as he listened.

Ten minutes later, the detective sat back in his chair, hands locked behind his head. "Part of me can't believe it . . ."

"Believe what?"

"That Emma Sanderson may be implicated in two murders . . ." He paused, checking his watch. "Colbie needs to know—if she's available, I'll ask her to swing by." Another pause. "You're invited, of course . . ." Dellinger grinned, motioning for Baldwin to sit. "You did a good job today—if my gut is right, we'll have this wrapped up within the week."

"A week? A rather lofty goal, don't you think?"

Damion shook his head. "Nope—I can feel it. This whole thing stinks, and with the info you got today?" He hesitated, wondering where their new lead would carry them. "Well, let's just say, I don't think Emma Sanderson has the stomach for this sort of thing . . ."

Baldwin's eyebrows arched. "Oh, I don't know—she sounded pretty experienced to me. It was clear she didn't have much use for Maxwell after she spilled her guts about talking to you . . ."

"True. But, here's the real question—why? If she's involved in either murder?" Again, Damion paused. "What does she have to gain?"

Baldwin said nothing, thinking of possible answers. "I agree with you, Sir—it doesn't make sense."

Dellinger checked his watch, then fired off a quick text to Colbie and, within seconds, she answered.

"She's on her way . . ."

CHAPTER 24

The human spirit is an interesting thing—it soars, dives, then soars again, especially at the pinnacle of perfection. To some, an indomitable spirit is the one, defining thing in their lives—others? They could care less. Emma Sanderson?

Nothing was going to stand in her way, and 'spirit' didn't have a damned thing to do with it.

A woman many considered a Georgia peach proved otherwise, her mercurial moods more than most could endure—it was, in fact, the sole reason she never married. In retrospect, however, living life sans a husband was just fine with her—fewer irritations that way. It was a choice she made early on, never regretting it a day since, and it certainly proved a way to augment the one thing important to her . . .

Cash.

The truth few knew? Emma Sanderson was a woman who cared for nothing but herself—and, she'd always been that way. With few friends throughout her life, an impenetrable façade always got her where she wanted to go—with the exception of fame, of course. Although, there were those within her circle often claiming Emma should have been on the stage because of her ability to morph into anyone she wanted to be. A changeling of sorts . . .

Honestly? It was more than a little creepy. Friends she managed to keep for more than a week or two dwindled to a mere two or three by the time she graduated college with a useless liberal arts degree—at least, that's what Richard called it. Diploma in hand, once she began managing the family tobacco farm, business tanked, many in the family blaming her for its eventual demise—somehow, that was easier than scrutinizing the overall tobacco market to pin the blame.

Emma, however, was having none of it. With a slicing tongue and venom to match, she finally alienated everyone who cared for her, including her brother. By the time he left for his first, major dig, their relationship deteriorated to the point of insincere cordiality, neither wanting their time together to last long. So, when Richard discovered the Mayan statue?

An opportunity she couldn't resist.

Delighted for an open door to pursue a fuller life with laser focus, it was then Emma Sanderson began to make plans. But, of course, if she were to exact them to perfection, she needed help—and, it didn't take her long to figure out the two, least likely accomplices. She didn't know them personally at the time, but, with the last name of 'Sanderson,' those within Richard's network accepted her without question. One thing she learned?

Money talks.

Brief introductions behind them, Detective Baldwin cued the surveillance file, Colbie listening intently, glancing once or twice at Dellinger. "I have to say I'm completely stunned . . ."

Damion nodded. "I'm with you . . ."

"The question is why? What would Emma Sanderson have to gain." She paused. "And, are you thinking she was involved in Richard's murder?"

"Not to mention Ramskill and Nathan Moss . . ." Baldwin focused on Colbie. "What do you think?"

"I'm not sure—but, from this tape, she's sure as hell's involved in some way. There's no disputing that . . ."

Damion was quiet, thinking of their next play. "She knows we're on to whatever it is she has going . . ."

"When you interviewed her, what did Peyton say about Emma?"

"Not much. Apparently, Maxwell wasn't privy to much information . . ."

Colbie nodded. "The perfect pawn."

"Exactly . . ."

Colbie sat back in her chair, images beginning to form in her mind's eye. "Like I said before—there's someone else."

"What do you mean?"

She glanced at Detective Baldwin knowing what she was about to say wasn't going to be popular. "Emma Sanderson isn't the one . . ."

"You mean she didn't murder Ramskill, or Moss?"

Colbie nodded. "Or, Richard . . ."

Baldwin glanced at his boss. "How do you know?"

Assuming Damion explained her abilities, she wasted no time with an answer. "Because the principal energy associated with the murders is male . . ."

With that comment, Dellinger cycled through his conversations with her. "You never said that before . . ."

"That's because it's only being revealed to me now."

"Why is that," Baldwin asked.

Colbie turned to him, smiling. "I wish I had the answer, Detective Baldwin—but, I somehow receive information at the time I need to know it."

"You didn't need to know it before now?"

Detective Dellinger shot a look at his subordinate. "I'm sure Baldwin didn't mean that the way it sounded . . ."

"I know—but, honestly? I don't blame him. It's difficult to understand . . ."

Damion nodded. "Moving on—if Emma Sanderson didn't off her brother, Ramskill, and Moss, then who did?"

"I don't know—but, I was just shown one other thing."

"Care to share?"

"Peyton Maxwell played you like a fiddle . . ."

Silence.

It was one thing to know a case wasn't moving along as it should—it was quite another to be played for a fool. "Meaning," Dellinger asked, embarrassment rising in a florid flush.

Colbie noticed. "Don't blame yourselves—I'm convinced Peyton Maxwell knows exactly what she's doing. And, coming to the precinct? All part of her plan . . ."

Dellinger's stomach lurched—not from what Colbie was saying, but from the realization he was dead wrong when it came to the archaeologist.

A punch in the gut.

"So—where do we go from here," Baldwin asked.

Colbie hesitated, not wanting to eclipse Damion's authority. "That's up to your boss . . ."

It was a class move, one not unnoticed. "We haul Maxwell back in—and, this time, it won't be pleasant."

"May I make a suggestion," Colbie asked, waiting for his answer before continuing.

"Of course!"

"Well—what do you think about my taking a crack at Emma? After her visit with Peyton, she has to know we're on to her—or, if we aren't, we soon will be."

"Good point. You already have time with her under your belt, so maybe she'll confide . . ."

"I doubt that—from what I heard on the surveillance file, she's a completely different woman than the one I met when we were just getting started. I suspect the person we just listened to has serious, pathological issues . . ."

So, for the next hour they planned, each leaving with renewed vigor for the investigation. Baldwin wasn't quite sure what to make of Colbie, but, he had to admit she made sense. What bothered him?

Peyton Maxwell taking his boss for a ride.

CHAPTER 25

None would've pegged Peyton for a coward—so, when she decided to get the hell out of Dodge, it was best to do so without the agony of tearful goodbyes. Those close would question why she'd leave a good job with benefits and academic perks, and inquiries would be difficult to answer. So, an early morning getaway seemed the best choice, leaving family and friends to always wonder. If someone asked, of course she'd lie, making up something they'd probably believe—but, if they didn't?

That was on them.

Packing up her apartment wasn't an issue—always a minimalist within her own space, she preferred her personal life to remain unfettered. Uncluttered. Uncomplicated. It used to be that way, too, until her life spun out of control when Professor Richard Sanderson showed interest. There was something about him she particularly enjoyed, his quiet nature always offering a sense of calm in what was usually a chaotic, academic world.

Unfortunately, it was for reasons unexplained why he decided to answer the archaeologist's call of the dig. Clearly, he had much to gain by staying stateside, proving his claim the Maya migrated north as far as Georgia. Never wavering, he endured what many called 'wishful fancy,' staunchly defending his position even more so after his discovery.

For a while, that's what Peyton thought he was going to do—you know, stand his ground. But, on a warm, spring day when Sanderson suddenly announced he was heading for the place of his dreams?

Well, in Peyton's mind, something seemed skewed.

Off.

Naturally, others noticed. It was obvious Richard's being in the public eye no longer held an allure and, in fact, his demeanor shifted from confident to questioning—in more ways than one. Although he was quiet, he loved to talk, engaging in philosophical discussions about a time he'd never known. So, when he began to withdraw, everyone turned a blind eye, saying nothing.

Peyton was certain Sanderson's behavior was the topic of conversation behind closed doors, and she couldn't blame them. To her?

Richard Sanderson seemed a broken man.

By the time Colbie turned the key to her room, the day had taken its toll. Although Damion figured they were on the right track—until she mentioned Peyton Maxwell played him for an idiot—she thought otherwise.

A quick shower later, she curled up on the love seat, a towel wrapped around her wet hair, hot chocolate in hand. Fluffing the pillow behind her back, she settled into the couch's comfort and closed her eyes, asking her guides to step forward.

Allowing her body to drift into meditation, she recalled the words of the spirit guide who'd been with her since she was a little girl . . . *ask and listen.*

And, that's exactly what she did. *What is it I need to know about Peyton Maxwell,* she asked, feeling herself sink deeper into a pleasing, meditative space. Sometimes, answers appeared as symbols, brief images, or spoken words within her brain—but, when she asked about Peyton Maxwell?

Much more.

Although brief, suddenly Colbie was a passenger in the back seat of Maxwell's car, watching as the archaeologist threw luggage in the trunk, climbed in, then sped down the highway. *She's running . . .*

Eyelids fluttering, the scene suddenly changed to a place she didn't instantly recognize, yet it was familiar. *Where is it?*

In a guided response, seconds later the footage slowed, finally stopping on its message. As if she were staring at a still-life painting, her guide's answer floated into her mind's eye—a small statue of what appeared to be a native warrior wearing a necklace tinged with fading blue. *The statue Richard Sanderson discovered!*

Without warning, a brilliant silver flash prompted Colbie to pull back, jerking her violently from the solace of meditation. As her eyes opened, Detective Dellinger stood before her, then vanished.

Damion!

Twelve or so hours really wasn't enough time to fully digest the consequences of Peyton Maxwell's actions. So, when Colbie pulled up to Emma's farmhouse early the following morning, Sanderson was less than pleased. The last thing she needed was being on the hot seat without the proper amount of time to devise a new plan. "How nice to see you," she greeted Colbie, her smile insincere. "It's early for you to be this far out in the country . . ." Emma held the front porch screen door open, stepping slightly to the side. "Please—come in!"

Colbie returned the smile, crossing the threshold into the farmhouse kitchen reminding her of her grandmother's. "I know it's early—but, at least I beat the traffic!" As if she were in her own home, she pulled out a chair, making herself comfortable at the table. "I adore country kitchens," she commented, careful not to focus directly on Emma. "I can see why you live all the way out here . . ."

Emma sat across from her, well aware she should offer her guest a cup of coffee or tea, but decided against it even though she had one of her own. To do so would surely imply she had time to listen to whatever it was Colbie was there to dish up. "So, what can I do for you?"

"Well, we're making progress, and I wanted to tell you in person . . ."

"I'm afraid I don't understand—is this about Richard?"

Colbie eyed her with obvious intent. "In a way—but, that's not why I'm here."

"Then . . ."

A soft sigh. "I suppose it's best not to beat around the bush . . ." Colbie paused, noting Emma's knuckles whitening slightly as she gripped her coffee mug. "I'm aware Peyton Maxwell paid you a visit yesterday . . ."

"Peyton? Well, yes . . ." It was all Emma could say as she quickly realized there were only two reasons anyone could have known about her conversation with Maxwell— either Peyton told Colbie or someone close to her, or she was wearing a wire. "I'm afraid I don't understand . . ."

Colbie smiled, sitting back in her chair, crossing her legs casually, hands comfortably in her lap. "Oh, I think you understand just fine, Emma—you know your conversation with Peyton Maxwell yesterday was less than heartwarming." She paused, her words pinpricks to Emma's conscious. "So— knowing that, you're probably assessing your position."

"My position?"

Another smile. "Yes—as of now, you're in a precarious situation, and you have a decision to make."

"And, what decision is that?"

"Tell me about your involvement with your brother's murder—and, the murders of David Ramskill and Nathan Moss. Or, don't, and deal with the consequences later . . ."

"Excuse me?" Emma's tone turned icy, her eyes dark. "I don't like what you're implying!"

"Oh—I'm not 'implying' anything. I'm stating directly I know you have a hand in what happened to your brother, as well as his colleagues . . ."

Without question, it was a cards-on-the-table moment, something to which Emma was unaccustomed. "My! How you've changed since we first met . . ."

"I'm sure I can say the same about you," Colbie said with a cynical smile, noticing a thickening tension in the air. "You stand at a crossroads, Emma—and, as I said, you have a decision to make." A pause. "So, what will it be?" Of course, Colbie knew damned well Emma was about two hairs on a spider's leg from throwing her out—but, it was worth a try.

Suddenly, Emma stood, pointing dramatically at the door. "Get out!" Hers was an unpleasant screech, one which Colbie didn't want to hear again.

"I take it you choose to take your chances," Colbie commented, not moving.

"I said, 'Get out!'"

Slowly, Colbie stood, taking her time knowing she was infuriating Emma Sanderson with each second. "I'll inform Detective Dellinger of your choice. I'm sure he'll be in touch soon . . ." With that, Colbie brushed past her, intuition in high gear. "Who's the man I see in your life, Emma?" A pause before opening the screen door. "Someone I know?"

She didn't wait for answer. Emma stood silently as Colbie let the screen door slam behind her as if a statement of things to come. Watching as she drove down the lane, there was only one thing on Emma's mind . . .

It was time to take matters into her own hands.

Peyton scanned the small living room one more time, her hand resting slightly on the door latch. *I think that's everything*, she thought, making sure she had her laptop bag. Suddenly, a loud, impatient rap on her door caused her to step back, heart racing. Quietly, she stepped up to the peephole, peering into the face of the one person she didn't want to see.

Clifford Rasmussen's eye met hers, yet he said nothing, knowing attracting attention to himself wasn't the ideal situation.

So, in that moment, Peyton had to decide and, without another thought, she opened the door. "Clifford! This is a surprise! Please, come in!"

Stripping off his driving gloves as he stepped across the threshold, he couldn't help but notice the travel case. "Going somewhere?"

Peyton smiled. "Only for the weekend—my best friend is having a bridal shower."

An answer Rasmussen didn't buy. "I'm surprised you have a best friend, my dear . . ."

Peyton's eyes narrowed. "What does that mean?"

"Nothing personal—it's simply you don't understand the meaning of friendship. So, how could you possibly hold a friend dear to you?"

"How dare you!" She bristled at his arrogance. "Say what you came to say, Clifford—then, get out!"

Several paces into the room, he turned, glaring at the woman who chose to defy him. "You're in no position . . ."

"No position?" Peyton's sweet smile morphed into a scowl. "Perhaps you forget, Clifford—I know everything! It's you who's in no position . . ."

Rasmussen motioned to one of the living room chairs. "Shall we?" Not waiting for an answer, he sat in what he knew was her favorite, placing his gloves carefully on its arm, straightening them so they were perfectly even. "We have much to discuss . . ."

Another decision to make.

If she made a fuss, someone would surely hear—and, drawing attention to herself was exactly what she didn't need. "I have to leave in five minutes," she finally answered, sitting in the chair across from him.

"Time isn't an issue, my dear Peyton . . ."

"Then, say what you have to say, and get out . . ."

Clifford simply looked at her as if trying to make up his mind. "You know, Peyton—as I sit across from you, I realize I may have made a mistake." Suddenly, he stood, motioning for her to join him. "I apologize for the intrusion—you have places to go and friends to see!" Heading for the door, he placed his right arm around her shoulder, giving her a light squeeze. "Please accept my apology . . ."

"Clifford . . ."

Peyton's words caught as a hot, searing pain ripped into her chest. Slowly, she crumpled, eyes wide with horrified realization, blood beginning to stain her freshly pressed, white linen shirt.

Then, a final, gasping breath . . .

CHAPTER 26

No one had a clue until Damion sent two uniformed officers to haul Peyton Maxwell in for a second round of amped-up questioning three-and-a-half days after Rasmussen stealthily left her apartment. After knocking several times, Officer Brad Kirkland pointed to a small stain on the door jamb. "Is that what I think it is?" He glanced at his partner, then leaned down for a closer look. "Blood . . ."

Officer Benson glanced at him, then the door. Drawing his weapon, he assumed a ready stance to the side as Kirkland knocked loudly. "Miss Maxwell?"

Nothing.

One more time. "Miss Maxwell?"

Again, nothing.

Benson's hair rose on the back of his neck. "See if there's a manager on site," he suggested. "I'll wait here . . ."

Within five, Kirkland returned, apartment manager in tow and, seconds later, the two officers stood over Peyton's body, both scanning the room—it was obvious she'd been there for a few days, and the likelihood of anyone's being around was nil.

"Call it in. Then holler at Dellinger . . ."

"It's happening," Damion commented, smiling, as he poured Colbie a glass of merlot. "It's almost over! I think . . ."

Colbie raised her glass. "To the end of this case! I'm ready to head back to Seattle!" She smiled, noticing the look in his eyes. "What about you?"

He pulled back slightly. "What do you mean? Am I ready for you to go back to Seattle?"

Colbie smiled, yet said nothing, curious about how he would answer.

"If that's it, then the answer is no—I think we work together pretty well." He paused, not taking his eyes from her. "But, I know you have to go . . ."

"For the first time in this case," she admitted, "I'm ready to move on—I have no doubt Emma Sanderson has been pulling the strings. But, what I still don't understand is the pile of leather you found by Moss's body—what happened with that?"

"Ah! Good question—and, your timing is perfect. Results hit my desk this afternoon—they were, in fact, journals. And, you were right about their not being expensive—probably thirty bucks tops on Amazon."

Colbie sat back in her chair, holding the wine glass lightly in her fingertips. "Aha! I knew it!" She paused, thinking. "That opens things up . . ."

"Meaning?"

"Well, if there were only leather for one journal, I would think it well could have been Moss's . . ."

"And, since there were enough for several?"

"Then, in my mind, that means he was keeping journals on other people—not just Tabashi Abnal. Something tells me they weren't all about him . . ."

"Holy crap! You're right! With everything happening, I didn't think twice about Moss's trying to blackmail him!"

"So, if that's the case—who else was he shaking down?"

"Okay. To make sure I'm getting it . . ." Damion paused, organizing his thoughts. "You're saying Nathan Moss was keeping journals on other people for blackmail purposes—right?"

Colbie nodded. "You have to admit, it makes sense . . ."

A nod. "It does. But, as you just asked—who was he blackmailing? And, why?"

"The main players in our investigation . . ."

"We have several—so, who's at the top of the list?"

"For starters, Peyton Maxwell—she lied to you, and I have no doubt she's in this up to her eyeballs." Colbie paused, recalling a previous conversation with Dellinger. "Didn't you say you were going to pick her up for another round of questioning?"

Damion nodded. "Funny you ask—my guys should be doing exactly that as we speak." At that moment, his cell buzzed and, checking the screen, he motioned to Colbie, then left their table to speak privately. Minutes later he returned, grabbing his coat from the back of his chair. "We can cross Peyton Maxwell off our list . . ."

"What?"

"My boys just found her in a pool of dried blood right inside her apartment door . . ."

Knowing their suspect list just got shorter, Colbie figured Dellinger had his hands full, and she was on her own—at least for the next few days. After diving into Emma Sanderson's background, only a few searches alluded to a broken relationship with her brother, one seeming to pick up on a certain animus between the two.

Even so, there was little to link her to her brother's murder, prompting the thought of a second conversation with Dr. Marian Summerfield.

A phone call later and within a couple of hours, she again sat across from the respected archaeologist. "I appreciate your seeing me on such short notice," Colbie began. "A lot has happened since the last time we met . . ."

"I heard—such a shame."

"It is . . ." Colbie took a second to get a handle on the room's energy—there was a negativity she didn't understand as she decided where to begin. "I know, of course, you knew Richard Sanderson and David Ramskill—but, I'm curious. How well did you know Nathan Moss?"

"Nathan? Not at all, really—all I know is he worked at the university with David Ramskill." She paused, casting her eyes downward as if thinking about something important. "We didn't travel in the same circles . . ."

"That makes sense . . ." Again, Colbie sensed a heavy energy. "Did you ever have the chance to meet him?"

"A couple of times . . ."

"Do you recall where?" As soon as Colbie asked the question, Dr. Summerfield's eyes narrowed. "I'm just trying to figure out where Nathan was close to the time he was murdered . . ."

"Well, I'm sure I can't help you—the only time I saw Mr. Moss was at our conferences."

"The most recent conference?"

"Well, now that you mention it, yes . . ."

"I was there—I recall seeing him, but I don't remember seeing you!" Colbie smiled. "But, it was crowded . . ."

"It was—Clifford said it was the best conference within the last ten years!"

"Clifford? Rasmussen?"

Instantly, Dr. Summerfield realized her uncustomary lack of judgment. "Yes—he always sends out a newsletter after every conference. This year, it appears, we outdid ourselves!"

Colbie paused, instantly recognizing an opened door. "He's been involved in Mayan artifacts for years, hasn't he? I mean, when I met him at the get-together before the conference, he was the man everyone tried to talk to— including me! Bernie introduced us . . ."

"Well, you're certainly right about that . . ."

"I imagine you've known each other for years . . ."

"Oh, yes! Clifford and I went to the same university . . ."

"Really? How interesting! Was he always involved in artifacts?"

"Yes, and no—it wasn't until after he graduated did he express an interest in Mayan culture."

"Did you reconnect then?"

"Reconnect?"

"Yes—well, I assume after you graduated, you didn't see each other. You know—going your separate ways." A pause. "Although, now that I hear myself, it's a silly assumption!"

Dr. Summerfield smiled. "You're correct—it wasn't until he became respected within archaeological circles as a viable collector did he gain an elevated reputation."

Colbie smiled, pausing for effect. "Well, as interesting as all of this is, I should probably get to the reason I wanted to meet with you today . . ." She leveled a serious look. "I think all of this revolves around one thing . . ."

"And, what is that?"

"The statue . . ."

"The one Richard Sanderson discovered . . ."

"Yes—is there a history to it?"

Dr. Summerfield thought for a moment, unsure of what Colbie was asking. "You mean a legend?"

"Exactly!"

"Well, not really—although, there were many in the Yucatan who said an apparition of the warrior would suddenly appear out of nowhere, especially on jungle trails."

"Did it appear for any particular reason?"

Dr. Summerfield nodded. "Also according to legend, those who saw it, suffered great tragedy not long after . . ."

"What kind of tragedy?"

"Death, mostly . . ." The archaeologist smiled, noticing the look on Colbie's face. "But, it's only legend . . ."

"A disturbing one!"

"Yes, it is—and, according to the same legend, anyone in possession of the relic would meet the same fate." A pause. "That's if the relic were authentic . . ."

Colbie was quiet, recalling her first conversation with Dr. Summerfield. Although Sanderson brought the statue to her for authentication, Colbie couldn't recall her actually mentioning it was the real thing. "Was it?"

"Authentic?" Dr. Summerfield sighed softly, shaking her head. "Unfortunately, no."

Again, Colbie cycled through their first conversation. "Oh! Then, I must have misunderstood . . ."

"Misunderstood what?"

"Well, the first time we met, I recall your saying the statue was valuable . . ."

An obvious misstep. "Oh, it is—but, not as valuable as an original."

It was then Colbie recognized the cloying scent of unfinished business. "Did Professor Sanderson know?"

At that moment, Dr. Summerfield glanced at her watch. "I'm afraid I've run out of time, Ms. Colleen . . ." She stood, clearly indicating her intent. "If there's anything else . . ."

Colbie, too, stood, offering her hand. "I appreciate your time . . ."

Minutes later, she sat in her car, recalling every word of her conversation with the respected archaeologist. Tapping her cell, she clicked Damion's number to send a text. *Meet for lunch?*

Within seconds, an answer.

One o'clock? Same place . . .

CHAPTER 27

*N*atasha Ramskill sat across from Detective Damion Dellinger, her back straight against the unforgiving metal chair. No surprise—when news hit the wires Peyton Maxwell wound up six feet under, there was little doubt it wouldn't be long until the cops came calling.

Gloves on.

"I appreciate your coming in," Dellinger began. "I'm hoping you can clear up a few things . . ."

"What things?" She didn't take her eyes from him, her glare one of tedious boredom.

Detective Baldwin glanced at his boss, feeling him bristle from across the tiny interrogation room. "Before we get started, Mrs. Ramskill, would you like a bottle of water?"

Natasha nodded, never giving a thought to how her answer may come into play—it also never occurred to her to say thank you.

Dellinger nodded to Baldwin, then waited until the door closed before continuing. "I'm sure you've heard about Peyton Maxwell . . ."

"Of course I heard—it's plastered all over the news." Clearly, there was no love lost between the two, and it was doubtful Natasha shed a tear.

Damion sat back, making himself comfortable. "The fact you met with Ms. Maxwell not long ago places you as a person of interest . . ."

"Person of interest?" Natasha's eyes flashed, feigned indignation as unbecoming on her as it is on everyone else. "Why? I didn't kill her!"

"Convince me . . ."

"Why should I?" Suddenly, she paused, realizing her tenuous position. "She had a relationship with my husband, I admit—but, that's not reason enough to kill her!"

Dellinger nodded. "I agree—it isn't. But, Mrs. Ramskill, both of us know this is about much more . . ."

"More? I don't know what you're talking about!"

Dellinger glanced at the door as Baldwin entered with the customary bottle of water, twisting the cap as he handed it to Natasha—a subliminal incentive to drink.

"Who killed Richard Sanderson, Mrs. Ramskill?"

"Richard? How the hell should I know!" Irritated, she took a gulp of water, not bothering to replace the cap.

"How about Nathan Moss?"

Another gulp. "I have no idea . . ."

"Your husband? Surely, you have thoughts concerning the circumstances of his murder . . ."

Then, the signal Damion waited for in every interview he conducted. Natasha's shoulders sagged and, after one more gulp of water, she slowly replaced the cap, setting the bottle to her right. After a moment, she looked at Dellinger, then at Detective Baldwin. "I want immunity . . ."

"I can't promise . . ."

"Then, I'll go to my grave with a secret on my lips . . ."

It wasn't the first time Detective Dellinger had to make such a decision. Offering transactional immunity could gain him the information he needed—if not? He could still nail her on charges unrelated to her testimony. "I'll need to talk to my people—but, I think we can work something out."

Natasha straightened a little, a sense of accomplishment plumping her confidence. "I want it in writing before I say anything . . ."

Damion glanced at Detective Baldwin. "I may be a few minutes . . ." With that, he left the room, leaving Mark with a woman who regretted nothing. "I don't think you did it," he commented. "But, you know who did . . ."

Natasha glanced at him. "I said I didn't. I don't know how much clearer I can be . . ."

A shrug. "Unfortunately," the detective continued, "that doesn't make much difference in the eyes of the law."

A pause. "My boss didn't mention it, but, unless you tell us everything, the offer's off the table . . ."

It didn't take a genius to figure out what Baldwin was saying—spill her guts, or face life in the big house.

Pretty cut and dried.

Watching from the two-way mirror, Detective Dellinger noted every expression. Every move. "She's almost ready," he commented to an officer also monitoring the interview.

Moments later, he again sat across from her, telegraphing nothing. "First, let me be clear, Mrs. Ramskill—if we offer full immunity, and I learn you're not being forthright?" He hesitated, gauging her response. "I'll prosecute you to the fullest extent . . ."

Natasha said nothing, weighing her options. Finally, her eyes met his. "Deal."

Damion nodded. "Do you need to take a quick break before we begin?"

She nodded. "Thank you . . ."

While Detective Baldwin accompanied Natasha to the ladies' room, Damion shot off a text to Colbie. *Change of plans. Dinner at 7?*

Seconds later, his cell screen illuminated.

See you then . . .

The only place Clifford Rasmussen truly felt comfortable was a room surrounded by his treasures and success. The room where he could puff his chest with deserved arrogance.

His inner sanctum.

Never allowed to cross the threshold, his wife didn't dare enter for it was where he did his best thinking, always careful to make certain he maintained a predetermined level of decorum.

Her company was something he didn't need.

Carefully, he warmed a brandy snifter, then poured a Grand Marnier, thoughts turning to . . . well, everything. Would he have done things differently? *Probably*, he thought as he took a seat in his favorite chair.

Such an admission was one he rarely made, but the truth was he felt a flicker of remorse about Peyton Maxwell. Obviously, she was caught up in something she couldn't handle, although she was mistakenly confident thinking she could. But, when it came down to it?

She was in over her head . . .

Always one to recognize weakness in others, Rasmussen knew Peyton's ultimate mistake was her need for emotional comfort, as well as someone who would listen. So, when Richard Sanderson made his interests known? She jumped at the chance to claim a place on his arm.

But, Rasmussen knew it would never work.

Probably the only person who knew Professor Sanderson for what he was—spineless and malleable—it would be a lie to say Clifford sanctioned Richard's relationship with Peyton. He didn't—but, in order to achieve what he wanted and needed most?

She was perfect.

Introducing them proved an advantageous idea and, when he realized he could take care of business in more ways than one, he also understood time waits for no one. Honestly, if it weren't for David Ramskill poking his nose where it didn't belong, there was a good chance he might still be upright and breathing. *It was too much to ask,* Clifford supposed as he sipped his drink, thinking of how quickly things spiraled out of control. Although, if confessions were, indeed, a cleansing of the soul, he was the first to admit taking care of unfortunate business didn't bother him, at all.

And, Nathan?

Completely necessary.

You were a stupid, stupid man, he thought, thinking of Moss's audacity when confronting him with the trilogy of leather journals.

Suddenly, he plucked his cell from his pocket, tapping the screen to life—two more taps, and the call connected. "We have to meet . . ."

"We agreed . . ."

"There is no choice."

Silence.

"No choice, at all . . .

"You look exhausted . . ."

"Thanks—I hope I wear it well!" Damion sat back in the booth, washing his face with his hands. "It was a long day, and it's only the beginning . . ."

"Natasha?"

He nodded, focusing all of his attention on her. "What about you?"

"Well, I figured you were going to be tied up for a while, so I decided to see Marian Summerfield again . . ." Colbie paused, recalling the conversation. "It was weird—when I walked in the door, her office felt . . . heavy."

"Any reason why?"

"No—but, I did wonder if I were picking up energy from the huge number of artifacts she had."

"That makes sense—did it stay with you after you left?"

Colbie shook her head, then took a sip of wine. "Nope—it was only there." A pause. "I'm sure it was nothing . . ."

"I know what you mean, though," Damion agreed. "Some places have bad juju . . ." He glanced at the front door, then scanned the restaurant as any good cop would. "So—what did you talk about?"

"Well . . ."

"Oh, great! That sounds promising," he grinned.

"Richard Sanderson—and, the statue." She hesitated, knowing what she was about to say would throw a wrench into their investigation. Eyeing his glass, she returned the grin. "You should probably order another drink . . ."

"That doesn't sound good . . ."

"It isn't—she said the statue Sanderson discovered wasn't authentic."

Damion stared at her, hoping he misunderstood. "Are you kidding?"

"I wish I were," Colbie responded, shaking her head.

"But—didn't she authenticate it?"

"Yes—the first time I talked to her, I asked if the statue were valuable. And, she said it was—but, when I pressed her for a number, she refused." Colbie paused, thinking. "But, today? She said it was valuable, but not as valuable as the real deal—again, tap dancing around a solid number."

"Wait—something doesn't make sense. Why would she authenticate the artifact when Sanderson took it to her to corroborate his discovery?" He paused. "And, did she actually say it was real the first time you met with her?"

"No—just valuable."

"Was she lying the first time?"

Colbie didn't take her eyes from him. "Well—that's the question, isn't it?"

For the rest of their time together, conversation regarding the case continued, both thinking there was still information to discover. By the time they parted company?

A new plan.

"What are you doing here?" Emma peered at Natasha through the kitchen screen door, yet didn't offer entry.

"We have to talk . . ."

Taking a moment to consider what good a conversation with Natasha Ramskill could possibly do, finally, she relented. "Make yourself at home . . ." She turned, leaving her guest to open the door herself.

Of course, right then, Emma was in a rather precarious position—clue Natasha in on Colbie Colleen's visit? Or, keep her mouth shut in case things should turn. "I don't know what we have to talk about . . ."

Obviously, the latter.

"Well, for starters, how about my afternoon of being grilled by Detective Damion Dellinger?"

Emma said nothing, listening.

"Second—I made a deal."

"You did what?"

"Just what I said, Emma! I made a deal to save my own skin! This whole thing is going south, and you know it!" A pause, but one without tears. "I'm sure as hell not going down because of you!"

"You mentioned me?"

"Of course, I mentioned you!"

Emma was quiet, looking curiously at Natasha. "I can't quite believe you were that stupid—but, you certainly must be because you came here to tell me about it." A pause. "So, I'm wondering . . ."

"I'm here because I wanted to warn you! You have time to get the hell out of here!"

"And, go where, Natasha?"

"Who knows? Who cares? Surely you have the money to start over . . ."

Emma glanced out the kitchen window, focusing on the lane leading to her house—she had to admit, Natasha Ramskill had a point.

The truth was Emma Sanderson was beginning to tire of the whole damned thing—she never would've wanted any part of it until Clifford Rasmussen entered her world. He was, without doubt, the only man who showed her attention over the last—well, decades—and, she liked it. Certainly, she had the same right as anyone to enjoy her life and, when opportunity presented itself, she figured she could milk it for all it was worth.

Initially, what she didn't understand was why such a well-respected man would have anything to do with her. It weren't as if he flew under the radar with no one to notice he was keeping company with someone other than his wife. Although, to be fair, according to Richard, there was circumspect speculation the happy couple was on the skids well before Sanderson headed to the Yucatan.

Yet, being married for twenty-seven years didn't seem to dissuade the art collector in the least. He did, however, insist he and Emma were never to be seen in public, and all secret trysts must remain private—and, that was okay with her.

The fewer people who knew of the man in her life, the better.

But, when Clifford began introducing her to people in whom she had no interest, her curiosity piqued. And, when he suggested a plan to secure the statue Professor Richard Sanderson discovered, sell it, and split the money in spite of the risk?

Well, it wasn't until Richard wound up with his eyes pecked out, lying on a jungle trail did she fully understand the obvious reasons for Clifford's attention. Underhanded? Definitely. Did Emma care?

Nope.

A small price to pay for a few moments of joy.

CHAPTER 28

Although it crossed her mind to take care of business herself when Natasha Ramskill showed up on her doorstep, Emma figured it more prudent to discuss any appropriate action with Clifford. So, though he was stopping by to discuss other things, she figured it was the best time to discuss what had become a pesky problem.

"It's been a while," she commented as she poured two glasses of chardonnay. "You look tired . . ."

"I didn't come to talk about my sleep habits," he barked, irritation beginning to creep. "We have a problem . . ."

"Indeed, we do . . ."

He eyed her, recognizing the double entendre. From the time he walked in her door, he felt a heaviness—thickness—in the air. "It's come to my attention," he continued, "local authorities are beginning to look in our direction." He paused, knowing he must enact his plan without hesitation. "As much as Natasha aided us by guiding her husband to us to be the perfect patsy, I'm afraid her worth is rapidly depleting . . ."

"I could've saved you the trip," Emma commented with a smile. "Although, I must confess it's much more pleasant this way . . ."

"Saved me the trip?" A pause, eyebrows arched. "I take it you have something to tell me . . ."

"Only that Natasha Ramskill paid me a visit before you called."

"A brazen thing to do . . ."

Emma agreed. "That's what I thought—but, as it turned out, it was advantageous."

"Explain . . ."

"Unfortunately, it seems she decided to accept Detective Damion Dellinger's invitation for a chat . . ."

A glare. "And?"

"She threw me under the bus . . ."

"She did what?"

Emma's eyes met his. "A unacceptable thing to do—and, it's clear she has to pay the consequences." She hesitated, thinking of what must be done. "So, it seems we have the same thing in mind . . ."

Clifford Rasmussen sat for several moments, quickly revamping his initial plan. "We have little time . . ."

Emma agreed, then asked the question he didn't want to answer. "You mentioned the authorities—why?"

Suddenly, he stood, then headed for the door. "Keep your mouth shut if anyone comes calling . . ."

Just before eleven, Colbie climbed into bed, ready to relax—if that were possible. Shortly after she and Dellinger parted after dinner, she again realized she forgot to mention the apparition of him a few evenings earlier. *Maybe it's best,* she thought as she plumped the pillows, settling into their comfort.

Sleep, however, proved elusive as she tried to sweep away recent information regarding their investigation. Her conversation with Richard's sister did nothing to dissuade Colbie's belief Emma wasn't to blame for her brother's—or, Ramskill's—murder. Even so, she clearly had knowledge of something. *Someone talked her into it,* she thought as her eyelids finally grew heavy. It was then she heard a familiar whisper. "You stand at the platform of the Kingdom of the Snake . . ."

Then, a silent thought.

Remember the seasons . . .

Clifford Rasmussen rarely deviated from a well thought out plan, possessing an 'everything has its place' mentality, one driving his wife nuts for the last twenty years. So, when her husband began to act out of sync, she noticed—bringing it to his attention, however, was ill-advised. Rarely did he pace and, when he did, it usually had something to do with work. That morning?

Something was up.

"Will you be working on your book today," she asked, pouring his coffee, knowing full well he hadn't worked on it in months.

Though he could have done without conversation at all, Rasmussen figured answering her question was the least he could do. "No—not today. I have errands, and I'm afraid I'll have little time to write."

"Errands? Anywhere special?"

"No—just work." He patted his mouth with a white, starched napkin from the linen service, then rose, heading for the foyer. "Don't expect me for dinner—it's going to be a long day."

With that he was gone, leaving his wife to wonder . . .

Quickly, she grabbed her jacket and headed for her car, waiting until he pulled from the drive, then began pursuit. What she expected, she wasn't sure . . .

She did know, however, there was something.

Knowing his daily tradition came in handy as she kept out of sight when he stopped at a coffee shop for a skinny latte, and a danish. With a perfect view, she watched as he pulled out a chair, settled, and took a few bites, checking his watch more than once. *Obviously, my dear, you're expecting someone...*

Ten minutes in, Rasmussen's wife watched as he stood, instantly recognizing the woman in a tan trench coat with an umbrella hooked on her arm. *Natasha!*

Of course, barely knowing her, there was no obvious reason he should meet her surreptitiously—if, in fact, that's what he was doing. Having met her a few times at society functions, Clifford's wife figured there was little they had in common—she was nothing more than a pretty bauble on her husband's arm. *Still, there must be something...*

Keeping her eye on them from the car, she watched as they finally left the shop together, heading for her husband's car. As any gentleman would do, he opened the door for her, but, to his wife, it seemed out of obligation rather than affection. In that moment, she realized Clifford was as cold with Natasha Ramskill as he was with her. *This is something completely different...*

Pulling into heavy traffic, it was only minutes until she lost them, leaving Rasmussen's wife to wonder about her husband's destination. *Whatever you're doing,* she thought as she pulled into the garage, *it isn't good...*

Only days after his men found Peyton Maxwell blue and waxy in a pool of blood on her apartment floor, Detective Damion Dellinger stood just inside the front door, hands on hips, scanning the room. "They have to be here . . ."

"What, Sir?" Detective Baldwin, too, glanced around the living room, unsure of what piece of evidence his boss was seeking.

"The journals . . ."

"You mean like the ones Moss had?"

Dellinger nodded. "Exactly—it doesn't track he was only blackmailing Tabashi Abnal. There has to be more to it . . ."

"That makes sense," Baldwin agreed. "Who do you have in mind?"

"Well—dead bodies are stacking up, so we're starting there."

"Do you think he had journals on Maxwell?"

"I don't know—but, we're sure as hell going to find out!" With that, he directed his men to go through everything in Peyton's apartment. "If they're here, we'll find 'em . . ."

With Peyton's penchant for minimalistic decorating, it didn't take long—within twenty minutes, a uniformed Georgia officer rifling through a small closet emerged, three leather journals carefully placed in large, plastic evidence bags. "Are these what you're looking for," he asked, showing them to Dellinger.

With a smile, Dellinger glanced at Detective Baldwin. "Exactly—excellent work!"

Evidence in hand, Damion left the scene, leaving his second in command to oversee whatever else needed to be done—then, he called Colbie. "We just picked up three leather journals from Maxwell's place . . ."

"Seriously? Where were they?"

"In the back of a closet . . ." He paused, thinking about Peyton's apartment, his hand resting lightly on the bagged journals. "It was weird—when my guys found her, it was clear she was leaving town." Another pause. "If Moss were blackmailing her with the information contained in the journals, doesn't it make sense she would've destroyed or packed them?"

"One would think—but, maybe she forgot. You did say they were in a closet . . ."

Damion was quiet for a second. "Well, we won't know anything until I get eyes on the contents—I didn't want to go over anything at the scene with others keeping watch, if you know what I mean."

"Baldwin?"

"And, others." Damion checked his watch as he climbed into his car, then pulled into traffic. "Stay tuned . . ."

As with any police investigation, there's a lot of jumping down rabbit holes, only to emerge again with less than when initially taking the dive. But, when things go right?

There's nothing quite like it.

Seeming as if test results took longer than normal, word finally came down from on high that the blood spot found on the door frame of Peyton Maxwell's apartment was Clifford Rasmussen's, placing him squarely in their crosshairs.

"It's making sense," Damion commented, fishing out a last French fry from the bottom of the takeout bag. "He's been under our radar for too long . . ."

Colbie smiled, listening, as he rustled through the sack. "But, why? Why would he go to the trouble of murdering a bunch of people within his own circle?" She paused. "It's just stupid!"

"It certainly seems like it would be the first place we'd look . . ."

A momentary silence. "But, we didn't . . ."

It was a revelation neither wanted to consider, and the irony wasn't lost as they recalled past months with little to show for their efforts. The bottom line?

Neither Colbie nor Damion presented their work in the best light.

"Okay, Ms. Masterson—Detective Baldwin advised me you have information for us." Dellinger didn't take his eyes from the young woman sitting across from him as Baldwin took his customary stance behind her, facing his boss.

"I know I should have come sooner . . ." A sniffle. "But, when I heard Peyton was murdered—well, I was scared."

Damion sat back in his chair to appear as casual as possible with the thought of making her feel more at ease. "Well, the important thing is you're here now . . ." He waited, quickly realizing she may need a little subliminal prompting.

Luckily, he was wrong. "A few weeks before Peyton was murdered, she called me."

"Was that unusual?"

Christine Masterson shook her head. "No—we were best friends since college. But, it was what she wanted to talk about that was weird . . ."

"And, what was that?"

"Some guy who was trying to blackmail her . . ."

With that, Damion sat up a little straighter as Detective Baldwin shot him a knowing glance. "Did she mention the guy's name?"

"No—all she said was he'd been spying on her for a long time."

"Was that all?"

Again, she shook her head, dabbing at her nose with a wadded up tissue. "No—she said he kept a record of everything. From his spying, I mean . . ."

"A record—you mean like journals?"

"I guess so—Peyton didn't say. All she told me was she had to do something to get them from him . . ."

"What did that mean?"

Christine was quiet for a moment until a cold look settled in her eyes. "She . . ." A hesitant pause. "Well, you know . . ."

Damion scooted forward, leaning forward on his desk. "Do you mean she had a relationship with him?"

A nod.

"So, you're saying Peyton Maxwell had a relationship with the person who was blackmailing her—is that correct?"

Another nod.

"For what purpose?"

"To get the records—or, whatever it was he wrote."

Dellinger glanced at Baldwin. "Did she?"

"I think so—but, I don't know for sure. She sent me a text a few days later telling me 'mission accomplished.'"

"And, you think she was referring to getting the records from the guy who was blackmailing her . . ."

"Yes . . ."

A heavy silence descended, Damion and Detective Baldwin understanding how Peyton Maxwell managed to have the journals in her possession. As Dellinger discussed with Colbie, it made no sense for a blackmailer to leave the goods with the person he was shaking down. "Was that the last time you heard from Ms. Maxwell," he asked.

"Yes . . ."

So, for the next thirty minutes or so, the questioning continued until both detectives were satisfied they learned all Christine Masterson had to offer. Baldwin went about his business, leaving Damion to connect with Colbie, bringing her up to speed. "We talked about it, but, when we found the journals at Maxwell's apartment, I didn't put two and two together as to why she'd have them . . ."

"Well, it makes sense. And, that makes me wonder if the reason Moss were lying next to journals with the pages torn out . . ."

"Someone wanted to get their hands on them . . ."

"And, I think I know who . . ."

Damion smiled, knowing they were thinking the same thing. "Rasmussen . . ."

"Yep . . ."

A tightening noose is never a good sign, and Clifford Rasmussen knew it. Once thinking he took care of all possible ragged ends, he realized it was a mistake to think the person most likely to do his bidding wouldn't turn on him.

Emma, as it turned out, wasn't thrilled with the idea of possibly spending her remaining years in the clink, giving it great consideration after Clifford left the last time she saw him. The question was what she going to do with the information she knew Georgia's finest wanted—and, after long and careful thought, intelligence pointed her toward throwing everyone under the bus, including her paramour.

Saving her own skin was tantamount.

So, when she invited Detective Dellinger to chat with her at the farmhouse, of course he couldn't say no—what he insisted on, however, was Colbie's sitting in on whatever it was she had to say. The time for coddling was over, and the more intimidating Emma Sanderson found them, the better. "I appreciate your coming here on short notice," she commented as she poured three cups of tea. "It's clear I've gotten myself into something I never intended . . ."

"We've all done so . . ." Damion glanced at Colbie, both instinctively knowing things were about to fall into place.

"Perhaps—but, probably not to this extent." Emma paused, surveying the kitchen table to make sure they had everything they needed before cleansing her soul. "I have quite a story to tell . . . "

Colbie took a sip of tea, then placed the cup in its saucer. "Take your time, Emma—and, for what it's worth, Detective Dellinger and I know what you're about to share with us is difficult for you"

A nod, then a brief silence. "When I met Clifford Rasmussen . . ."

Turning the carefully folded piece of paper in his fingertips, Clifford Rasmussen stared out the window, watching evening city lights twinkling in twilight. Dealing with Natasha proved more difficult than anticipated, yet, when he convinced her it was the right thing to do, she was wise enough to concur.

Even so, things got messy.

Then, opening the small bit of paper he again read, noting the numbers were, indeed, a combination. Although not regarded the sharpest knife in the drawer in the academia world, Rasmussen knew David Ramskill was bright enough to hide the Sanderson statue if he were, in fact, the one who kyped it after the archaeologist's unfortunate demise.

Of course, he grilled Natasha about it before—well, before doing what had to be done—and, by the time she drew her last breath, there was little doubt she was as much in the dark as he. Realizing the numbers were a combination, there was nothing to point him or her in the direction they needed to go. *You weren't that bright*, he thought as he read the combination from left to right, then in the opposite direction, hoping for a disguised clue.

But, after careful and close scrutiny there was nothing.

Until Clifford Rasmussen realized the answer was right under his stuffy, relic-collector nose.

CHAPTER 29

As much as she knew she had to save her own ass, Clifford Rasmussen's name rolled off of Emma's tongue easier than she initially anticipated. With only a few, targeted prompts from Detective Dellinger, she spilled her guts about everything like a canary waiting to warble. "It's no secret there was no love lost between the two," she commented, directing her attention squarely on Colbie.

"Why?"

"Because of Richard's ability to find what others could not—it was nothing more than greed."

"Surely, Clifford Rasmussen was a force in his own right within the art relic world," Colbie probed, "so, you're saying it was nothing other than money motivating him to steal the statue . . ."

Emma nodded. "As soon as Richard shared his discovery with Clifford—before the public announcement—Clifford knew immediately it was worth a fortune. Richard thought so, too, and that's why he sat on a formal press release of his discovery."

Damion's turn. "What doesn't make sense is how Clifford managed to coerce everyone to help him get the statue into his own hands . . ."

"Oh, but it does!" Emma smiled, as if recalling a fond memory. "He promised all of us money!"

"Did he give you a figure?"

"You mean how much all of us stood to make?" Emma hesitated, frowning. "Now that I think of it, he didn't give exact figures—but, he said the statue was worth well into seven figures."

Damion scribbled a few notes, mostly to remind himself of what questions he needed to ask—he didn't want to forget a thing. "Who exactly was involved in your plan?"

"And," Colbie interjected, "what was the plan? Obviously, it was to steal the statue from Richard . . ."

Emma nodded. "That's right—after Richard took the position at the Yucatan dig, there were only a handful of people who knew my brother would take the statue with him."

"Meaning, only a handful knew it would be in a safe . . ."

"Yes—if you recall, we talked about that when you first knocked on my door."

"I remember quite well . . ." Colbie's tone chilled slightly. "It was quite a tale you wove . . ."

"I had no choice," Emma agreed, although there wasn't a speck of remorse or contrition.

"What part did you play?"

"The simplest, really—it was up to me to make sure Richard had the statue safely secured when he went on the dig."

"You suggested he take it with him?"

"Well, of course! How else could it work? If he didn't keep the statue in a safe—like he always did—there would be no opportunity for David to steal it!" Emma pulled her head back as if surprised by Colbie's naiveté. "It really was a perfect plan . . ."

"Did he?"

"Steal it?"

Colbie nodded, glancing at Damion.

"Yes—but, that happened before Richard's murder. Not after . . ."

Damion kept quiet, allowing Colbie to take the reins— as he listened, he couldn't recall a witness as cold as Emma Sanderson.

Colbie paused, unsure if she heard correctly. "Wait— you're saying David Ramskill stole the safe before Richard was killed? If that's the case, how is it Richard didn't notice?"

Emma chuckled. "Well, it weren't as if he was checking his safe every day . . ."

"Then, he had to have had the combination . . ." Damion didn't look up as he took more notes.

In that instant, Colbie realized how David Ramskill could have stolen the ancient relic without Richard's noticing. "You gave him the combination, didn't you?"

Another soft chuckle. "Of course! I made it a point with Richard—if something happened to him, it only made sense for me to have the combination."

"Wasn't he suspicious?" Colbie looked at Damion, then returned her attention to Emma. "From what I understand, you weren't exactly the best of friends . . ."

"That's true—but, somehow, we managed to mend the fences before he left for the dig." A pause. "And, he agreed it made sense . . ."

Detective Dellinger flipped a page in his notepad, then focused on Emma. "Okay—so, Ramskill lifted the statue out from under your brother's nose. Then why did someone hear and see him at Richard's cabin . . ."

"It was a shack, Detective. Let's call it what it was—a ramshackle room with barely four walls. To call it anything else would be a travesty . . ."

"Okay—duly noted. But, you haven't answered the question . . ."

"Clifford Rasmussen ordered him—that's how Nathan Moss got involved."

"Tell me . . ."

Suddenly, Emma rose, taking her teacup to the kitchen sink. "David figured it would be smarter to send someone who was under the radar . . ."

"In other words, Ramskill threw Moss under the bus . . ."

"Exactly—if he got caught, it really didn't matter. Nathan was expendable—or, so we thought."

"Meaning?" Damion's full attention was on the woman whose blood ran cold.

A sigh. "The journals, Detective—we had no idea Moss was keeping journals on us."

"You, as well?"

"That . . ." she admitted, "we don't know. Moss never came to me with his pet project like he did Peyton and Clifford . . ."

Curious she didn't mention Abnal, Damion thought as he listened, Colbie having the same thought. "Have you heard of Tabashi Abnal," she asked, pen poised.

"I've heard the name—why?"

Colbie didn't extend the courtesy of an answer. "Who killed your brother, Emma?" Colbie looked at her expectantly, as a mother would a guilty child.

"David Ramskill."

Then, Damion. "Who killed Nathan Moss?"

"Clifford."

"Who killed Peyton Maxwell?"

"Clifford."

The thing about uncomfortable silence is once it digs in, it's there to stay. The clipped precision with which Emma delivered her answers was disconcerting for Colbie and Damion, both feeling an uncomfortable chill as she continued to answer their questions. "Did you help him?"

"If you're asking if I were present, the answer is no . . ."

Again, Colbie was quiet as Damion continued. "According to Dr. Marian Summerfield, the statue Richard discovered wasn't authentic—and, she told him so. Is that accurate?"

"Maybe—it was one of the possible reasons Richard decided to work at the dig. If it ever got out his life's best discovery was nothing more than something created as an art project, his career would have been ruined . . ."

Colbie and Damion said nothing, noticing Emma's face turn dark as if recalling her worst nightmare. "It is unfortunate Richard met his maker before knowing the truth . . . "

Damion didn't take his eyes from her. "The truth?"

"Yes, Detective—the truth."

"And, that is?"

Emma paused dramatically, the performance she was presently giving the best of her life. "That statue, Detective?"

Damion said nothing.

"It's real . . ."

CHAPTER 30

As you might imagine, after Emma's tell-all, it wasn't long until Detective Dellinger hauled Clifford Rasmussen on the carpet. Subsequent to Damion's and Colbie's time with Sanderson's sister, there was no question Rasmussen would be a guest of the state for the rest of his days—not exactly what most would consider a fitting culmination for a respected career. The icing on the cake? Rasmussen's self-perceived, golden opportunity to throw Dr. Marian Summerfield as far under the bus as quickly as possible. A deflection? Of course. Anyone who knew him, would expect nothing else.

An issue of character, don't you think?

Damion certainly thought so. "It's unfortunate we meet under such circumstances," he commented, opening his tablet with two pens clipped to the top page. Early in his career, he discovered they offered a subliminal message that he was going to be writing a lot of things down, making it easier to catch one in a lie.

"Before we begin," Dellinger began, his voice definitive, "I feel it fair to advise you—you're here regarding the murders of Peyton Maxwell and Nathan Moss." He looked up, focusing on the man sitting across from him.

A momentary silence as Clifford Rasmussen gathered his thoughts. "It is, indeed, Detective Dellinger, unfortunate my colleagues met an untimely demise. However, I assure you I had nothing to do with either . . ."

"Then, it seems we're at odds—I'm clear about your position, and I'll appreciate your cooperation. Truth will be a favorable component of our conversation . . . "

"I have nothing to hide . . ."

As usual, Detective Baldwin, stood behind and slightly to the side of their suspect, keeping a wary eye, listening to everything. He and his boss were used to bald-faced lies, both knowing they were going to hear a few doozies from the illustrious art collector.

And, so it began.

"Let's begin with Peyton Maxwell—how long did you know her?"

Rasmussen eyed the detective, his demeanor cool and detached. "I knew *of* Ms. Maxwell when she first completed her master's degree."

"When was that?"

"Probably seven or eight years ago—she was quite the talk of the archaeology world, and that's how she came to my attention."

"Did anyone introduce you?"

"Not really—she attended our conferences over the years, but, interestingly, this year was notable because of her absence."

"Do you know why she didn't attend?"

"Oh, please, Detective—why would I know something such as that? I barely knew her well enough to call her by her first name . . ."

Time to switch gears. "What about Nathan Moss? Did you know him well enough to call him by his first name?"

"Nathan?" Rasmussen paused a moment, a bemused smirk tugging at his lips. "Nathan Moss was a pathetic excuse for an archaeologist . . ."

"I take it you didn't care for him . . ."

"It wasn't that I didn't care for him, Detective—he may well have been something to someone. Unfortunately, his career never took off, and he shape-shifted into someone none of us recognized."

"Shape-shifted how?"

"Well, as I understand it, his metamorphosis began several years ago—before David Ramskill took him under his wing."

"David Ramskill?"

"Yes—everyone within my close circle knew Ramskill was looking to elevate his status within our tight community.

Many considered him one who would always walk in Richard Sanderson's footsteps, yet it was clear Ramskill was vying for attention."

As Rasmussen spoke, Detective Dellinger filed mental notes, briefly questioning to himself why Rasmussen spoke like a stuffy English professor. "Did he ever reach such a pinnacle in his work?"

"Ramskill? Good heaven's no—he simply wasn't capable. And, it didn't help when his colleague discovered one of the world's greatest artifacts . . ."

"You're referring to Richard Sanderson's discovering the Mayan statue?"

"Who else, Detective?" Rasmussen threw him a look of disdain, as if he were barely able to be around someone of such lowly stature.

Knowing they had much ground to cover, it was then Detective Dellinger quickly diverted from his original plan. With Rasmussen in such a talkative mood? It certainly behooved the good detective to hammer down on specifics—and, that meant tackling only one or two topics during the first interrogation. "Have you seen the statue, Mr. Rasmussen?"

"Only once, shortly after Richard's discovery."

"Did you have a chance to scrutinize it carefully?"

"If you mean did I have a chance to look at the statue closely, the answer is yes—and, no."

"Meaning?"

"I had it in my hands for a moment or two, but there was little time to look at it closely."

Then, the question needing corroboration. "Was the statue real?" *Who better to know of authenticity than a self-aggrandizing scholar,* Damion wondered, waiting for an answer.

"I assume you're asking if the statue were authentic . . ."

Dellinger nodded.

"I had my doubts . . ."

"Do you know if Sanderson had its authenticity verified by someone else in the archaeology field?" An elementary question to which Dellinger already knew the answer— Interrogation 101.

For Rasmussen?

Opportunity.

"I don't know for certain, but, if he were to do so, it certainly would have been authenticated by Dr. Marian Summerfield."

Damion took his time writing a few notes, then checked his watch. "Do you need to take a break, Mr. Rasmussen?"

He shook his head. "No—thank you. I have an important meeting this afternoon, so I prefer to wrap this up as soon as possible."

"Well, I'm not sure you'll make that meeting—would you like to take a few minutes to make appropriate calls?" As soon as the words came out of his mouth, he knew they were a mistake. If Rasmussen suddenly decided he needed legal counsel?

Dellinger would be SOL.

"But," he continued after a moment and in an effort to keep Rasmussen talking, "we'll see . . ." It was barely enough of a carrot to assure Clifford Rasmussen's arrogance was all he needed to guide the detective's thoughts in the right direction.

His direction.

With a slight nod, Damion continued. "Do you know Dr. Summerfield well?"

"Again, Detective, we're colleagues—in the academic world, relationships are secondary. Even on the personal friend level . . ."

Dellinger was quiet not because he was thinking, but for effect. Finally, he again focused squarely on Rasmussen. "Then, if that's the case—and, you say it is—why is it your blood was found on Peyton Maxwell's door frame? Surely, for you to be there, you must have had some sort of relationship."

He paused, allowing Rasmussen to take his time, the question an adroit maneuver to assure Damion remained in control. Clearly, Rasmussen was trying to direct the interrogation to something self-serving, but, in Dellinger's mind, it proved an elementary attempt, at best.

Clifford shifted slightly in his chair, then tugged on his shirtsleeve cuffs, making certain they were in perfect position—a gesture Dellinger noted. It was—for the first time in the interrogation—a minute, absent-minded motion indicating Rasmussen was becoming uncomfortable.

"DNA proves it's yours, Mr. Rasmussen . . ." Damion waited as that piece of news found its mark. "But, while you're thinking about that, why don't you tell me about the journals Nathan Moss kept on you, and Ms. Maxwell . . ."

"Journals?"

Damion smiled, fully aware Rasmussen was using every bit of feigned ignorance and innocence he could muster—and, it was always the part of interrogations the detective found amusing. "Yes—we know all about them."

Clifford said nothing, his mind recalling the pages he ripped from Moss's journals, watching them burn in the living room fireplace. In his mind, it was clear—Dellinger was fishing. "I have no idea what you're talking about, Detective."

Then, a little detective creative license. "Perhaps you're aware journals were found beside Nathan Moss as he lay face up in a dumpster . . ."

It was a description Rasmussen didn't particularly enjoy, but he did delight in the fact he knew the pages weren't included. "Did they mention me," he asked, his voice growing cold.

A question Detective Dellinger chose not to answer. "Are you aware Peyton Maxwell was the victim of Moss's journals, as well?"

No answer.

"And, Tabashi Abnal?"

Abnal? A name Clifford Rasmussen didn't previously consider—and, it was one that could cause him a great deal of trouble. If Abnal spilled his guts about setting up Richard Sanderson for David Ramskill?

Not good.

"I'm sorry, but I don't recognize the name . . ."

Bullshit, Damion thought as he began to grow weary of Rasmussen's arrogance—but, if he were to keep the relic art collector talking, he had no choice but to put up with it.

Another about-face. "Who do you think killed Richard Sanderson," Dellinger asked.

"I have no idea . . ."

"Surely, you have suspicions . . ."

Clifford Rasmussen crossed his arms, leaning back in his chair. "David Ramskill . . ."

Of course, there was no way Damion could ascertain whether Rasmussen threw Ramskill's name into the fray because that's what he actually thought—or, whether he were sticking to a preconceived story. His gut?

The latter.

"Why?"

"The reason is as old as time, Detective—jealousy. Richard Sanderson was the person David Ramskill wanted to be—and, he'd do anything to achieve what he thought he so rightly deserved. But, like I said, he wasn't capable . . ."

"Do you know for a fact David Ramskill murdered Richard Sanderson?"

And, there it was—the point in a conversation when one has the opportunity to tell the truth, or try to cover his own ass with a traceable lie. If he answered in the affirmative, he would be incriminating himself since the whole thing was Rasmussen's idea in the first place.

But, of course, he couldn't let Dellinger know that . . .

CHAPTER 31

By the time Damion had a chance to call Colbie, it was after seven, too late for an impromptu dinner. Besides, he had a headache—being around Clifford Rasmussen for the better part of a day was more than he could stand. "He is, without question, the most arrogant person I've ever had the pleasure to question," he commented when they connected via FaceTime.

Colbie chuckled. "You're right about that—when I met him at the gathering for the conference attendees, I needed fresh air after the first five minutes!" She paused, thinking about the relic art collector. "How far did you take him?"

"Well, he admitted he thinks David Ramskill killed Richard Sanderson because of jealousy. It seems when they worked together, it gave Ramskill plenty of time to figure out how he was going to take Sanderson out of the picture so he could assume the position of 'top archaeologist.' Whatever that means . . ."

"That does, however, go along with what Peyton Maxwell told me—and, the only reason she had anything to do with him was because of their plan."

"Agreed . . ."

"Did you hold him?"

Damion shook his head. "No—I have a feeling he's too arrogant to run. He thinks he's smarter than everyone else, so that plays into our hands . . ."

"Well, there's always the chance . . ."

"I know—but, I really don't think he will. I put Baldwin on him, so if he tries anything, he'll be burying himself." Dellinger paused, thinking of the direction he wanted the interrogation to go the following day. "He's supposed to be at the precinct at nine in the morning—so, we'll see."

Colbie watched as Damion leaned back in his chair, hands clasped behind his head. "The good news is he doesn't have any idea of what we know . . ."

Within ten, they clicked off, Damion ready for a hot shower, a beer, and a good night's sleep.

Colbie?

Not so much.

It's curious what twelve hours can do—while Damion welcomed his precinct guest with a smile and a handshake, Clifford Rasmussen wasn't quite so magnanimous. After having a few hours to himself reflecting on his conversation with Detective Dellinger, it was more than apparent his position was becoming increasingly compromised by the minute.

For Dellinger, that meant pulling answers was like pulling teeth.

"Did Baldwin have anything interesting to say about his surveillance last night," Colbie asked when she and Dellinger linked up for their usual synopses of the day.

"No—nothing out of the ordinary."

"What about Rasmussen?"

"It was a damned miracle he didn't lawyer up. Not too bright in my book . . ."

Images beginning to form, Colbie closed her eyes. "This is weird—I'm seeing a book, and it has the word 'prologue' on it . . ."

"What the hell does that mean?"

Colbie tried not to smile. "I'm not sure—but, I feel it's telling me something has yet to be done."

"How in God's name do you get that from the word 'prologue?'"

"Well, I'm looking at what's missing . . ."

Damion decided not to say anything, completely confused by the interpretation of her vision. He watched her eyelids flutter, and there was no question she was in her intuitive space.

"Pages are flipping from the beginning to the end . . ." As she watched pages fly by, it suddenly dawned on her. "There's no epilogue!"

"Okay. I'm totally confused . . ."

"Well, when a book has a prologue, it means it usually has an epilogue to tie things up—what I was seeing didn't have one!"

"And, that means . . ."

"We don't have the complete story!"

From the time Rasmussen left the precinct on his second day of questioning, Detective Baldwin kept a close eye. At first, there was nothing of interest to report—until shortly after nine o'clock that evening when Rasmussen pulled from his garage, heading toward the university campus. Within thirty, he parked, then walked directly to the archaeology department—why, Baldwin couldn't figure.

Nearly deserted, there were few to witness his arrival, making it much more difficult for the detective to maintain surveillance without detection. Even so, he kept his distance, listening to the art collector's footsteps echo as he climbed the stairs.

Waiting until they stopped, Baldwin followed, listening carefully. Tracking Rasmussen with only soft, corridor lights to guide him, he stopped at an office door, standing to the side, making sure he wasn't casting a shadow. From his vantage point, he noticed the door recently had a nameplate removed, concluding it was, most likely, David Ramskill's office.

Two minutes.

Five.

Then, a slight sound.

Quietly, Detective Baldwin peered around the door jamb just as Clifford Rasmussen extracted something from a small safe tucked among Ramskill's many relics. With a smile on his lips, he held it reverently for a few moments, then slipped it in his pocket. Quickly placing the safe and relics exactly as they were, he made certain their placement was perfect.

The statue! Realizing Rasmussen was preparing to leave, the detective quickly ducked around the corner at the far end of the corridor, listening and watching as Clifford casually left the office, then headed down the stairs as if he owned the place.

Within minutes, Baldwin was again on Rasmussen's tail, staying out of sight until he pulled into his garage, flicking off the lights. Baldwin watched as the living room drapes closed, preventing further surveillance, his gut telling him

Rasmussen was in for the night. *Dellinger needs to know about this,* he thought as he tapped his cell to life.

Then, a text.

Meet me at Rasmussen's . . .

"Hold on . . ." Damion checked his cell, then stood. "That was Baldwin—he said to meet him at Rasmussen's?"

"His house?"

He nodded, then looked into the camera as he shut his laptop. "You coming?"

"On my way!"

Arriving only five minutes after Dellinger, Colbie had no trouble spotting Rasmussen's place—parked down the street from his home, both men stood outside of their vehicles, Detective Baldwin bringing Damion up to speed.

By the time Colbie joined them, he had the full story. "It looks as if our missing statue is gone no more," he commented as she slipped the car keys in her jacket pocket.

"Seriously?" She glanced at Baldwin, then focused her complete attention on Dellinger. "Rasmussen?"

"None other . . ."

For the next few minutes he filled her in, then glanced up the street toward Rasmussen's home. "And, if he took that statue, he's probably getting ready to run—I doubt he'd leave it knowing it's worth a small fortune."

Colbie agreed. "I think you're right—if you don't move now, you may not have another chance."

"God knows he has enough money to go wherever he pleases . . ."

Plan concocted, Detective Dellinger called for backup—he didn't want to be caught in a situation that could quickly go south—Rasmussen was, after all, a two-time killer.

It wasn't, however, quite that easy.

Protocol dictated paperwork and waking a judge before putting the apprehension in motion, so it wasn't until shortly after two o'clock in the morning Detective Damion Dellinger pounded on Clifford Rasmussen's front door.

Waking in the dead of night must have addled his brain because Clifford Rasmussen opened the door before looking through the peephole as he fumbled with his bathrobe belt.

If he had, things might have turned out differently.

As it was, shortly after, he was on his way to booking to be charged with the murders of Peyton Maxwell, and Nathan Moss, leaving his wife stunned—but, not really. "Of course, those are the obvious charges," Damion commented as he and Colbie prepared to leave the scene. "There'll be a lot more, I'm sure . . ."

"More axes to fall, I suspect . . ."

"Emma, Dr. Summerfield, and Natasha . . ."

Colbie was quiet for a moment, the sound of Natasha's name sparking an ill-feeling. "Speaking of Natasha—she's been out of the picture a little too long.

That makes me nervous . . ."

CHAPTER 32

*Y*ou know how it goes—pull one from the corner, and the perfectly built house of cards will never stand. That's how it was when Clifford Rasmussen decided complete cooperation would play in his favor. Although the death penalty was rare in his state, the possibility of such a sentence remained, and taking a chance was nothing if not foolish.

Emma Sanderson and the prestigious Dr. Marian Summerfield felt the same way, each ultimately telling a different story in order to save their own skins. And, there was a good chance Natasha Ramskill would have felt and done the same simply based on her prior discussions with Detective Dellinger.

It wasn't difficult to predict—once Rasmussen started flapping his jaws about their involvement, it didn't take either long to lawyer up, both women standing in defense of themselves and each other. So, by the time Colbie prepared to return to Seattle, little was resolved, subsequent trials more than a year out.

"So, that's it—our 'epilogue' for all intents and purposes. According to Rasmussen, it was Summerfield's idea to squirrel the statue's authenticity for Sanderson—but, after his murder, not knowing its exact location threw a wrench into things." For the first time in months, Detective Damion Dellinger took time to relax, enjoying the company of someone whom he wished would stick around.

"No wonder she was so conciliatory when I requested time to speak with her for a second time," Colbie agreed, watching him slide a lime over the rim of his glass, then plop it into the ice-cold beer. "I don't think I told you when I first tuned into the case in the Yucatan, I heard a whisper . . ."

Damion gave her his full attention. "And, it said . . ."

"You stand at the platform of the Kingdom of the Snake."

"What?"

"At the time, I didn't know what it meant—but, later, I heard the phrase again, and something else . . ."

"Which was . . ."

"Remember the seasons—and, I think it was guiding me to Dr. Summerfield. She was the snake . . ."

"Summer—of course!" He paused. "But, by talking to you again, it was also a great way to find out how close we were to discovering her involvement." He grinned, knowing their case was about to wind up stamped and in the books. "What surprised me?" He didn't wait for an answer. "Natasha—Rasmussen didn't need to kill her."

Colbie's eyebrows arched. "Seriously? Of course, he did! He knew he could control Emma and Marian Summerfield, but Natasha Ramskill was another story. She was one tough woman . . ."

"Cold is more like it—and, even though Rasmussen says it was Dr. Summerfield's idea to tell Sanderson the statue was a fake, I'm not buying it. They were in it together, Natasha included . . ."

"Don't forget Tabashi Abnal—what are your thoughts on him?"

Although he didn't express it, Damion felt for the Yucatan archaeologist—he was duped into something he didn't expect. "I don't know—that's up to prosecutors. But, since he came clean about his involvement? They'll probably go lightly—besides, there's always extradition to think about, and they may not want to go that route. . . ." A pause. "It'll all come out at trial, and I'm sure Abnal will be in the mix."

"You're right . . ."

"It's kind of sad . . ." He sat back in the booth, soft light diminishing new lines etching the sides of his eyes. "And, thinking of Natasha—if we hadn't hauled Rasmussen in when we did, who knows how long it would have been before she was discovered."

"I know . . ."

"But, the good news is we have blood evidence on Rasmussen from Peyton's apartment . . ."

"Not to mention the blue paint inside Ramskill's and Sanderson's mouths—Rasmussen's calling card, although I'm sure he didn't expect us to figure it out."

It was then Colbie remembered her vision, and the evening Damion appeared for a brief second at the end of her bed. "You're never going to believe this—but, remember when we were really getting a handle on Peyton's involvement?"

"Yes—especially when she showed up at the precinct."

"That's right—well, it was around that time I had a vision of Peyton's packing, and leaving her apartment."

"Turns out that was relevant . . ."

"I know—but, what I didn't tell you was I also saw an apparition of you standing at the foot of my bed." Colbie paused, recalling the bright flash of light. "I kept forgetting to tell you . . ."

"Weird. What does it mean?"

"Well, I'm not sure—but, I also saw a brilliant flash of silver light. You know—like something shiny flashing in the sun."

Damion said nothing, equally aware of soft lamplight seemingly erasing all signs of stress on her beautiful face. "Peyton was stabbed, so maybe you were picking up on that—and, it was right at the time when she was at the top of our list."

Colbie thought for a moment, then nodded. "You're probably right . . ."

Time for another topic. "Enough business for the evening!" He hesitated, considering whether he should ask his question, but, curiosity got the best of him. "So—what about you? Where do you go from here—back to Seattle?"

Colbie matched his grin, lifting her glass. "Back to everything normal," she commented as their glasses clinked. "I think so—I'm beginning to miss the gloom of the West Coast. Besides, I have a few things I need to wrap up regarding my business . . ."

"Are you sticking it out?"

"I haven't made up my mind—I need to have a long conversation with Ryan and Kevin, then figure out what I'm going to do." She paused. "What about you? Are you planning to stay on the force?"

No answer.

"Really? You're leaving?" There was no doubt—Colbie could tell by the expression on his face he made a decision.

"I think so—I'm not ready to announce it yet, but after working with you and being the boss of my own time, schedule, and way of doing things, I realize I like it."

"It does afford a certain freedom . . ."

"I know—and, it's that type of freedom I need in my life. I spent too many years doing what someone else wanted me to do—and, the stress isn't worth it."

"Especially, if it's affecting your health . . ."

Damion laughed, taking a sip of his beer. "Another blood pressure spike is exactly what I don't need!"

So, for the next couple of hours they sat, each confiding thoughts they seldom shared with anyone. By the time the hostess informed them the dining room was closing, both knew their time together had come to an end. "If you're ever in Savannah . . ." Damion pulled Colbie close as they stepped onto the curb. "Be sure to look me up . . ."

As if it were the most natural thing in the world, she melded with him the way she used to with Brian. "You'll be the first to know . . ."

"Promise?"

A nod. "I promise . . ."

By Faith Wood . . .

the Colbie Colleen Cozy, Suspense Mystery Series

the Accidental Audience

Chasing Rhinos

Apology Accepted

Whiskey Snow

Chill of Deception

at the Intersection of Blood & Money

Scent of Unfinished Business

LAUNCHING IN SEPTEMBER, 2020!

Agenda!

Professional Acknowledgments

CHRYSALIS PUBLISHING AUTHOR SERVICES
L.A. O'NEIL, Editor
www.chrysalis-pub.com
chrysalispub@gmail.com

HIGH MOUNTAIN DESIGN
WYATT ILSLEY, COVER DESIGN
www.highmountaindesign.com
hmdesign89@gmail.com

Manufactured by Amazon.ca
Bolton, ON